MW00874886

Praise for

HEAR ME

"[A] moving middle grade novel."

—*The New York Times Book Review*

"This empathetic, appealing story highlights Rayne's journey to self-acceptance while also exploring her complicated but loving family relationships, loyal friendships, and a little romance."

—*Booklist*

"*Hear Me* is a thoughtful and empowering story about standing up and speaking out even when no one will listen. I'll be thinking about Rayne long after closing the book."

—Lynne Kelly, author of *Song for a Whale*

"*Hear Me* is a brave and important book. Rayne's story will open hearts and minds, and give young readers courage and hope."

—Jarrett Lerner, author of the EngiNerds series

"Kerry Cerra has written an important, immersive read filled with so much heart. We are quickly pulled into Rayne's world as she navigates her hearing loss journey from self-doubt to self-acceptance. I was cheering for Rayne every step of the way!"

—Danielle Joseph, author of *Sydney A. Frankel's Summer Mix-Up*

HEAR ME

KERRY O'MALLEY CERRA

CAROLRHODA BOOKS
MINNEAPOLIS

First paperback edition published 2024

Text copyright © 2022 by Kerry O'Malley Cerra

All rights reserved. International copyright secured. No part of this book may be reproduced, stored in a retrieval system, or transmitted in any form or by any means—electronic, mechanical, photocopying, recording, or otherwise—without the prior written permission of Lerner Publishing Group, Inc., except for the inclusion of brief quotations in an acknowledged review.

Carolrhoda Books®
An imprint of Lerner Publishing Group, Inc.
241 First Avenue North
Minneapolis, MN 55401 USA

For reading levels and more information, look up this title at www.lernerbooks.com.

Cover illustration by Robert Sae-Heng.

Main body text set in Bembo Std regular.
Typeface provided by Monotype Typography.

Library of Congress Cataloging-in-Publication Data

Names: Cerra, Kerry O'Malley, author.
Title: Hear me / by Kerry O'Malley Cerra.
Description: Minneapolis, MN : Carolrhoda Books, [2022] | Includes author's note. | Audience: Ages 10–14. | Audience: Grades 4–6. | Summary: "After being diagnosed with progressive hearing loss, Rayne resists her parents' efforts to "fix" her and rethinks her own assumptions about what her condition means for her" —Provided by publisher.
Identifiers: LCCN 2021060964 (print) | LCCN 2021060965 (ebook) | ISBN 9781728420745 (lib. bdg.) | ISBN 9781728460581 (eb pdf)
Subjects: CYAC: Deaf—Fiction. | People with disabilities—Fiction. | Self-acceptance—Fiction. | Family life—Florida—Fiction. | LCGFT: Novels.
Classification: LCC PZ7.C31927 He 2022 (print) | LCC PZ7.C31927 (ebook) | DDC [Fic]—dc23

LC record available at https://lccn.loc.gov/2021060964
LC ebook record available at https://lccn.loc.gov/2021060965

ISBN 979-8-7656-2692-4 (pbk.)

Manufactured in the United States of America
4-1011383-49307-6/12/2024

For Mom and Dad, who have always loved me exactly as I am and who were my ears when I couldn't hear.

And for Shawn, who helped me realize that even though my ears are broken, I am not.

CHAPTER 1

I climb inside the Box of Shame. Every time I do, I'm reminded again of how my dog, Lucky, must have felt with that giant plastic funnel stuck around her neck after she got fixed. Dad joked that it was her Cone of Shame. This giant metal box is mine.

My poor pup hid in the closet for days until her stitches healed, but at least she could hide. This box is the one place I can't fudge my way through. No changing the subject. No running away. No control. Just the truth, smacking me in my face, over and over.

That my ears are broken.

I'm broken.

The air is stale and makes me gag as I take out my aids, grab the chunky beige-and-black headphones, and fasten them over my ears. I don't even need the new lady in the white coat, Yvonne, to help. She looks a little older than my brother, Colby, but is definitely too young to be a doctor yet. I've probably done this more times in the last two years than she's had birthdays.

I sit on the only chair, facing away from the tiny, thick, scratched-up window, and count the holes climbing the metal walls in perfectly straight lines as Yvonne seals me inside. I only get to twenty-six before static, which I assume is actually words, buzzes in my ears, gradually getting louder until I can actually figure out what she's saying.

" . . . and *** repeat it to me."

I know.

I-know-I-know-I-know!

She's new. I'm not.

In this box, it feels like the whole hearing thing's being rubbed in my face, the same way kids in my class made fun of me when I botched the words to the R-Jarrow song last year in the Finish the Lyrics contest. Seriously, R-Jarrow's my idol. Everyone knows it. I should have won, but I had no idea the lyrics actually say *The guy will sing.* I've always thought they were *The sky will rain.* I looked it up online when I got home, and sure enough, that was the only line of the whole song I got wrong. And it wasn't like it was new. I'd been singing it wrong for over a year.

Whenever kids joked about me losing, it felt like a slap in the face, a reminder of what I no longer have. A lot like I feel now with Yvonne.

I really hope I can fake-pass this test. Maybe that will get Mom off my back, and I won't be stuck either looking like a Martian for the rest of my life, or living as a mime. Either way, it's a lose-lose situation—people are going to stare.

Yvonne says, "Say the word *airplane*."

From a shelf opposite my chair in the box, stuffed animals and a seriously creepy Mickey Mouse–like mask watch me. Like they're waiting for me to mess up. But this was an easy one. "Airplane," I repeat.

"Say the word *hurl*."

Not only do I hear the word, but I feel it. Deep in my belly. Every time I'm locked in here. Every time I'm forced to call on my nearly photographic memory by picturing the notebook I keep; it's filled with past words from this test. I write them down every time, as soon as I get out of this box. I try to memorize them, hoping—for once—they'll reuse some, so I—for once—can leave the Box of Shame without feeling stupid. But lately, to me, stupid feels synonymous with sudden hearing loss. "Hurl," I whisper, as my stomach clenches.

"Say the word *h*n*."

I flip through words stored in my head and beg the tears to stay locked behind my eyeballs. I pick a word I clearly visualize on page four. "Shone?"

Gripping the arms of the chair, I force myself not to turn around. Force myself not to plaster my eyes against the window to see if Yvonne has marked my answer right or wrong. But honestly, I don't need to peek. It's wrong. It was probably a *th* sound, not a *sh*. How do I confuse them?

I sit silently as my ears try to make sense of the next few words, but they don't. So I start guessing, because I have to make Mom believe I'm fine. Or at least prove that I'm not getting worse, because I'm not. I concentrate, closing my eyes, blocking everything out—even my own thoughts—and strain with all that's in me to hear the words. I can make out the word *vine*. I think. No, I'm positive. I repeat it. Then I hear *m**n*.

Come on, Rayne. Think. Vowels are not easy for me. But the *m*. I heard an *m*. The end sounded like an *n*. "Moon," I blurt, before the next word can fill the headphones, all while my heart pulls like a rip current.

I guess on a few more, knowing if this were a test in school, I'd definitely get an F. There's no grade for effort. With my eyes still closed, I imagine a perfect barrel wave curling over me, my surfboard carrying me out of this awful box, across the beautiful ocean to a deserted island where it wouldn't matter if I can hear or not because I'd be the only one there.

Yvonne yells through the headphones, "Now . . . you . . . are . . . going . . . to . . . hear . . . a . . . series . . . of . . . beeps."

Her voice booms so loud, it actually hurts my ears. I jump, and the creepy smile on that Mickey Mouse–like mask teases me. I want to tell Yvonne that she doesn't need to shout. And she doesn't need the volume cranked all the way up. But she must think I do since I most likely bombed the word test. She's probably thinking, *Poor girl! Surely she'll be all the way deaf by next week!*

Hurl. Hurl. Hurl!

"Yes, thanks. I know how it works." I'm hoping she won't finish the directions.

"Okay, um, here we go."

The first beep is loud and shrieky. As I push the clicker, I picture Mom and the stacks of printouts she downloaded from the internet to show Dr. James— as if he didn't already know all there is to know about cochlear implants.

No. Focus. Listen! Do not let Mom be right.

Click. I push the button. *Click, click.* They were beeps. They had to be. I close my eyes and concentrate as hard as I can. Yes, a beep. Low, but I'm sure of it. *Click!* Another? Was it? Did I make it up? *Click.* Again, yes, I hear it. *Click.*

Eyes sealed tight.

Click.

I hold my breath, not wanting to miss a near-silent beep.

Click.

Click.

Click.

I jump at the sound of Yvonne's voice. "Okay, sit tight for a second."

Easy for her to say. With no noise coming through the headphones, the tinnitus takes over. That constant loud ringing in my ears drives me nuts, especially at night when I'm trying to fall asleep. I look to the corner where two of the metal walls—the ones that cage me in—meet and try to distract myself by counting holes from the bottom up. This time I get to ninety-two before the vault door opens.

Yvonne's smiling as she takes the clicker from my hand. "Better than a shot at a doctor's office, right?"

I don't have my aids in, and though I can still hear certain things a little bit without them, Yvonne doesn't know this. So I pretend I have no clue what she's saying, especially because I'd take one hundred shots at a regular doctor's office over sitting in this Box of Shame any day. Her question is ridiculous. And mean.

She throws me that *I-feel-sorry-for-you* smile, the one people wear every time they find out I have hearing loss, and I wish I could erase it right off her face. I mean, if she's going to be an audiologist, she should at least be a better pretender.

I can faintly hear that she's still talking, but I don't look at her. I don't need to read her lips to know what she's saying: that for this next test, I don't have to do anything but sit still while the nearly upside-down, lopsided headband that hugs the back of my head tests something with my bones.

When Yvonne slips out and closes the door—before she gets to her side of the smudged window—I slide the headband backward about an inch. A test with no results is better than a test with bad ones. I close my eyes and mentally transport myself to my happy place, the beach, and prepare for Mom's scolding when Yvonne finally lets me out of this detention.

CHAPTER 2

Dr. James is examining the audiogram as I plunk onto the chair next to Mom. I pull out my notebook and try to write the five new words I saw on Yvonne's list when I stole a glance at it as I came out of the Box of Shame. *Youth. Beg. Jug. Phone.* Words I didn't catch. Words to memorize. Sounds and patterns to study, so I can figure out exactly what I don't hear in order to pretend that I do.

Before I can write the last word, *star,* Mom leans in and gives me a kiss on the cheek. Because she'd call this cheating for sure, I quickly flip to a new page and doodle my favorite star constellation— Delphinus—to help me remember to add the word later. Delphinus is a dolphin that, according to star lore, saved a famous ancient singer when he was robbed by pirates at sea. The singer jumped overboard before the pirates could hurt him. A dolphin heard the guy's song and rescued him, carrying him safely to land. The Greek god Apollo rewarded the dolphin with a constellation. It's one of my all-time favorite star stories.

Mom taps me. "How'd it go?" she asks me, but she looks to Dr. James for an actual answer. "I'm *** worried the last ear infection Rayne *** a few weeks ago damaged *** ears *** more."

Yvonne busted me on the bone test and made me redo it. I bet she told Dr. James. He gives me a tight smile. He probably also knows I guessed words and clicks. I *was* trying . . . maybe too hard. Part of me feels bad. He's a nice man, and I like him, but I'm sure I've wasted his time today. Those tests probably cost a million dollars, so I wasted that too. But he's not the one with a mom who, even though she can hear just fine, refuses to listen.

Mom's like a cat watching a game of ping-pong, looking from Dr. James to me and back. I turn away and hitch my left foot on top of my opposite knee and trace one of the constellations I drew on my sneakers. One boy called them dorky in the middle of the hallway at school, and a few kids laughed, but I'd rather them stare at my feet than my ears, so I keep wearing them.

Concern fills Mom's voice. "What's *** on? What's wrong ***?"

Dr. James clears his throat. "Nothing's *wrong*, Mrs. Campbell."

I lift my head, wondering if he's going to cover for me, because for sure, those tests get harder and harder each time. But maybe nothing has changed since last time. When all this testing started two years ago, I hardly had any loss at all. But Mom insisted she could tell something was seriously off. She kept bringing me back. And unfortunately, she wasn't exactly wrong. Every few months my hearing was taking a dive. I started praying every single day for a miracle that would fix me. I think it worked because things weren't that bad till last November. Now, I just pray it'll stop getting worse. I hold my breath and wait for Dr. James's answer.

"One test was inconclusive." He smiles at me, and I feel bad again about moving the headset.

"Should *** do it again?" Mom asks.

I wish I had a dolphin to rescue me from her.

Dr. James says, "Since you need official paperwork, we did." He points to the dip in the cookie-bite line on the audiogram. "But overall, Rayne's last testing was four months ago, and while there has been a slight change since then, she's still doing okay."

Dr. James is always positive. He has a way of making me feel like my hearing loss isn't a big deal at all, like I'm totally okay, and like I can live with it perfectly fine. But those thoughts don't follow me out the door when I leave his office. They don't follow me when I'm pretending to be the same old me in a world that's suddenly changed as fast as the afternoon thunderstorms come and go here in South Florida. Maybe I don't need a deserted island. Maybe I can just move into Dr. James's office. Minus the Box of Shame, I feel okay here. Like my ears aren't a big deal and everyone else who comes in is just like me anyway.

"Okay." Mom pulls out her phone to take notes. "I *** tell. It's only *** week into *** school year *** even her teachers *** *** struggles *** class. This *** why I told *** we're leaning toward *** cochlear implants. Is *** change in all the tests *** just one?"

"I wouldn't say the change is big enough to warrant you doing anything other than what you currently are," he says.

"Thank ***, but I *** need *** note which test had a change and what *** *** are so I can log ***."

She's flipping through the Notes app on her phone, ready to type in my latest failure. "I told my husband *** there is a change, we *** definitely *** the implants."

Implants mean surgery. A big one. Who wants their kid to have to go through that? Besides, I can hear fine, or mostly fine, with my hearing aids, and I can even hear some things without my aids in. There's no way I'm getting implants that'll bulge from the side of my head like the high-rise buildings downtown. I don't want to stand out even more than I already do. Before last year, before I first found out I was going deaf, surfing and student government were my everything. Now my daily everything consists of puzzling words together in my head, hoping that I'm getting conversations correct, and praying my aids won't draw attention by randomly screeching.

"Mom." I try to stop her. I'm pretty sure even Dr. James is tired of listening to her. "My hearing's not that bad. I don't need implants."

Without even turning up the volume on my hearing aids, I hear Mom exhale, and it's full of worry. But it only lasts a second, because she never wastes time—even the kids in her English class at school tell me this.

She says to Dr. James, "Rayne's hearing *** deteriorated *** quickly over *** last year, *** quicker than *** first anticipated, and cochlear implants *** *** only guarantee that she *** maintain *** quality of life. *** you agree? Dr. Olsen does."

"I'm not dying," I say. "I'm still me. Still Rayne." Those implants will change everything about me. "And who is Dr. Olsen?"

Mom says, "He's *** cochlear doctor I told *** I talked to."

"You never told me you were talking to a cochlear doctor!"

"*** must've forgotten. *** what do *** think, *** James?"

Dr. James says, "I *** *** agree *** Rayne here."

He always makes sure to talk so that I can hear him, but this time I missed a word. He said *have to*, right? It was definitely an *h* sound and a *v*. It didn't sound anything like *don't*.

He must notice my face trying to sort out his words. "Sorry, Rayne." He gives me a full-on smile and faces me so I can follow the conversation— another reason I'd love to move in here. "I said I do agree with you on this one. I don't want to get too far ahead of ourselves. Rayne is functioning quite well with the hearing aids, for now, even though her residual hearing is deteriorating. That gives you all plenty of time, and technology is changing quickly. Of course, implants are certainly a viable option when the time comes, but even those are evolving rapidly. Fully implantable—under the skin—implants are not far off. Surely Dr. Olsen mentioned that? Rayne will most definitely qualify as a candidate if her hearing continues down this same path, but I'm not sure she's there yet."

It's a total relief to hear him say that.

"And as I mentioned to you last time, I do believe stem cell research will make a breakthrough sooner than anyone expects, so it might not be long till that, too, is an option. It could potentially restore her cochlear hairs fully, and she'd regain at least some, if not all, hearing. The trials have been impressive. And until then, there are schools for kids with hearing loss, not to mention new hearing aid technology every year."

"Wait. There are stem cells that can fix my hearing?" I look at Mom, but she's reading one of her printouts. She's never mentioned anything about stem cells. I ask Dr. James, "How does that work? Is it painful?"

"We don't know much yet, but I imagine it won't be too invasive."

"Honey." Mom touches my hand. "We *** wait *** long. Dr. Olsen said *** longer *** go without hearing, *** less your auditory nerves *** be stimulated. So if *** time comes *** implants are *** only hope, it may be too late. Or it might take ten times longer *** you to be able to fully function *** them *** they're designed *** ***."

There is only one good thing about wearing hearing aids; I can turn them off whenever I want. And right now I want to, like I want to every time Mom starts heaving out her I've-done-my-research-and-it's-a-fact-that-cochlear-implants-are-the-best-*guarantee*-that-Rayne-will-ever-hear-normally-again. But I don't, because who knows what else Mom's "forgotten" to tell me. I need to pay attention.

"We *** count on stem cells or wait *** newer implants," she goes on. "The future *** them are too uncertain, and the research *** stem cell transplants shows *** at least ten years away. *** need help now, so *** don't keep falling behind *** school."

I wish I had a magic wand to zip and lock Mom's lips. Or better yet, I'd cast a spell to stop everyone from noticing my hearing problem at all.

But wait . . . if I had a wand, hello, I'd just wave my hearing loss away forever.

Mom turns to Dr. James. "*** used to be *** A student. And *** success rate for *** implants *** high, especially since *** oral skills are *** good. If we wait, *** *** actually hurt Rayne in *** long run."

"I fully appreciate the homework you've done on CIs, but I'm still of the mindset that she's not one hundred percent there yet. If you're worried about her falling behind, why not check out some of the schools designed for kids with hearing loss? There's a remarkable one in St. Pete. It'll give you guys some time."

Time. Yes. That would be great.

He reaches for a pamphlet behind his desk and slides it over to Mom. It says BAYVIEW SCHOOL FOR THE DEAF AND BLIND across the front.

She flips through the brochure, her hand touching her mouth every once in a while, before she pushes it away. "There *** *** enough change *** Rayne's life lately *** I think *** implants *** be the best bet to make sure she gets *** regular life back. A sense *** normalcy. Back to *** old self. Rayne doesn't need a special school."

I grab the brochure. The front side is all about the blind school, and the back is all about the deaf school. I mean, I guess they're the same place, but the information is divided up. I stare at the photos of the kids on the deaf side. They look . . . just like all the kids I know. I run my finger across one of the faces, inching closer to try to look at his ears, to see if he has a cochlear implant, but I can't tell. The picture's too small.

In my head, I can hear Mom's words, *special school*, like that's a bad thing, but if the kids there are all deaf, all in the same situation, maybe they don't feel "special" at all.

Dr. James comes from behind his desk and sits on the corner. "Here are the papers you need." He hands Mom copies of my latest tests. "I understand your concerns. Perhaps I could speak to Rayne alone for a minute?"

I suck in a loud breath and brace myself—hoping, praying that Mom might actually let me talk to Dr. James alone. I have a million questions I want to ask him. Like, does he agree that the stem cell thing is still ten years away? Will I go completely deaf before then? And what would he do if I were his kid? Would he let me have a say? My parents know I don't want implants, but Mom still goes on and on about how that's the best choice. How they'll help me feel like me again, and how they'll free me from the shell I've buried myself inside lately. Her words, not mine.

Mom looks genuinely surprised. "There's no need *** that. Rayne *** only twelve. I *** feel comfortable that she'd have *** discussion about *** without me present."

Just like that, my only chance to talk to Dr. James vanishes as quickly as Mom claims my hearing has. There's no point in fighting her. She never gives in. So I may not ever get to ask Dr. James the one question I want answered the most. The question that keeps my stomach in a knot every single day.

I want to ask Dr. James if Mom and Dad can force me to have the cochlear implants, even if I don't want them.

CHAPTER 3

I focus extra hard in class for the next few days, trying to prove to Mom and my teachers that my ears aren't getting worse. By the end of each day, I'm so tired from concentrating extra hard that I've been falling asleep early. Sometimes before I can even get my homework done.

On Thursday, instead of hanging out with my best friend, Jenika, after school before her volleyball practice, Mom makes me leave early, saying we have errands to run. She's listening to a talk show on the radio, which is so mumbled in my ears I feel like I'm listening to a foreign language, so I pull out my phone. Bluetooth connects my new high-tech hearing aids to the car radio, the TV, and my cell phone, so I can stream things right into my ears. Definitely a perk, though most of the time it just gives me more volume without really making the sounds clearer.

I'm surprised when Mom pulls into a parking spot at Pompano Beach.

"What are we doing here?" I ask. On the beach in front of us, Dad's kneeling near an old wooden lifeguard stand, fighting the wind to spread a blue-and-white striped sheet on the sand.

A tall, thin kid with shaggy blond hair is carrying three of our surfboard bags. He looks a whole lot like Colby, but there's no way it's him, right? He started his fall semester of college in Tampa a few weeks ago.

I watch him place the bags, fins up, on the sand. For sure, it's him. "Colby!" I yell.

A smile spreads across Mom's face. "Yep. He's home *** Sierra's birthday."

Colby and Sierra have been dating for almost two years, but she's only a senior in high school. They're trying to do the long-distance thing. The trip from Coral Springs to Tampa is only three and a half hours by car, but Sierra says it may as well be twenty. I guess she really misses him.

"Ohmygosh!" I practically bounce out of the car. "So where's Sierra?"

Mom closes her door. "I assume *** at cheer practice. *** see her later. Come ***, grab the beach bag I packed. It's *** *** backseat."

I grab the bag. It's stocked with towels, a football, and my hot pink bathing suit. Mom must have planned in advance, since we obviously left school together. This is the best surprise ever.

As we walk toward my dad and brother, Mom stops and hands me a ponytail holder. I hesitate to take it—I never wear my hair up anymore. I'm still getting used to all these changes, and I just want people to see me as the same old Rayne, not The Girl with Hearing Loss. Pretty hard to do when they stare at my perfectly curved aids hanging over my ears—flesh-toned in color doesn't mean invisible. Or when people laugh at my mistakes after I've heard things wrong. But here, I can make an exception. I take the ponytail holder and wind my hair through it, grateful for a nearly empty beach.

We used to come here all the time for beachnics—a word for beach and picnic that Colby and I made up when we were little. Colby hated homework, even though good grades came easy to him. Mom used the beach as an incentive to get him to do his assignments as soon as he got home from school. It always worked, because Colby loves surfing more than anything. Dad would meet us here, and we'd have Publix subs and get in some sunset surfing.

But we haven't had one at all since last spring, right before Colby graduated.

Dad tosses me a bag of white cheddar popcorn, my favorite. I smack it, slam-dunking the bag into our open cooler.

"Yes!" Dad yells. "Two points!" He high-fives me.

As soon as I drop the beach bag, Colby wraps his arms around me from behind, twirling me in a circle so fast I'm afraid my aids might fall out. When he finally sets me down, I turn and bear-hug him, partly because it's great to see him, but partly to steady myself.

"Welcome home," I say. I'm so glad USF's close enough for him to come for a weekend like this.

"Yeah, but don't get used to it." He leans in and whispers in my ear, "*** *** free *** great *** *** turn."

Based on the few words I could hear, I try to make out what he said—a giant puzzle in my brain. "It's free?"

He faces me and shakes his head, clueing me in that I got whatever he said wrong. He steps back, so I can read his lips. "Sorry, I forget sometimes."

In some ways, that's a good thing. I *want* people to forget I'm different. But in other ways, it's frustrating as all heck because I hate having to piece conversations together. Or guess what someone's saying. Or worse, flat out telling people that I can't hear.

Colby doesn't speak any louder, and since he whispered the first time, I'm guessing it's because Mom and Dad are standing nearby. But at least now I can make out the words he's mouthing. "Nothing against you or anything, but the freedom of being on my own is awesome. Wait till it's your turn. You'll never come back."

"I bet!" This sounds like a dream. If I were on my own, Mom couldn't make decisions about my ears for me. I'd totally rule my own world.

"Don't worry, we'll **ve plenty *** time together while I'm here," he says loudly, as we join Mom and Dad on the faded sheet. "I have a plan *** you to skip school tomorrow and hang with me."

Dad's in principal-mode, lowering his sunglasses and throwing Colby a piercing stare.

Mom reminds Colby, "Tomorrow's *** big election. *** can't miss ***, right?"

"Definitely not," I say. My whole family knows how important this is to me. For years, I've loved helping the student government kids at Dad's high school, and now in middle school, we have SGA too.

I was president last year, and I plan to win again tomorrow for seventh grade. Though I'm dreading the speech and everyone watching me.

Colby nudges me. "It was worth a shot."

It's awesome that he's here. Like just about every kid from Florida who stays in state for college, he started classes over the summer to get used to the school and the workload without a full campus of students around. Even though it was just a mini-semester, I missed him so much. Then he came home for two weeks, and things were back to normal, but once he was gone again, everything felt super hard. It's like he left right when I needed him most.

Mom passes out subs. Mine's dripping with oil and vinegar. Perfection.

Dad's got a mouthful of tuna on wheat, lettuce hanging from his bottom lip. As he shoves it in with his fingers, he mumbles . . . something. Usually, I have no trouble hearing Dad—something about his voice, or tone, or whatever—but I doubt any of us understood him with his mouth packed. He points to the surfboards next to us and repeats, "Sunset surfing. Like old times."

"Definitely," I say. Surfing's the one thing my family's always done together. I love it more than student government and equal to R-Jarrow—who, lucky for Jenika and me, is hinting at dropping a brand-new album very soon. I look to the ocean as the sun warms my skin. Minus the memory of the doctor appointment, it's a perfect day.

Near the water's edge, there's a kid sitting on the sand alone. Troy? My stomach flutters.

I stand. "I'll be right back."

I've known Troy since before I could walk. Our moms grew up together and are still best friends, but it's getting harder and harder to talk to him. Lately, he's definitely gone out of his way to hang out with me alone, but it feels weird. I mean, we've always just been friends. I don't know how to be anything different, especially since he keeps getting cuter and cuter.

I take my hair down to cover my aids. "Hey."

"Hey. What're *** doing here?" He moves like he's going to stand.

Before he can, I sit. "Colby's home, so we're having a beachnic. You okay?"

"***, fine." He looks toward my family. "*** good. I *** *** much *** *** Colby. Go hang *** ***."

The words scramble in my head, and I struggle to quickly make sense of what he's said. I heard "fine," so I'll just stick with that part and play off not understanding the rest. "You don't look fine."

He wipes the sand off the tops of his feet. "My mom dropped me *** while she's *** errands. *** debating *** online *** opportunity, *** this *** where I *** my best thinking."

Scramble. Scramble. "Sorry. What kind of opportunity did you say?"

"Oh, sorry." He turns to face me. "That better?"

My cheeks grow hot as I nod—embarrassed that he even knows to do this for me.

"A business opportunity."

"Whoa, Mr. Professional!" I try to get out of my own head by joking with him. "What can a kid our age even do online?"

He talks extra loud. "*** see, I happen to be a world-class gamer, and I find myself quite entertaining too, so I could probably make *** money *** streaming myself playing."

I laugh. Hard.

"What? Don't *** find me funny?"

"Not at all," I say jokingly. "But for real, people pay money to watch other people play games?"

"All *** time. But it costs money up front *** get equipment *** stuff. *** I have to hope *** some sponsors. It's possible that *** hysterical *** I am, I still may not get *** followers."

"Why do you need to? Why not just play for fun?"

He's quiet for a minute, then says, "I *** my parents *** having money issues, though they won't tell me *** sure. But I *** sense it."

"Oh, I'm sorry."

He shrugs. "My swim club's expensive, *** I was going to quit, *** my coach keeps saying I have potential to swim *** free in college if I keep at it. So even *** it costs *** lot now, I could save my parents *** in *** end. I figure *** I can cover my own club fees, it's *** less thing *** them to deal ***."

"That's really nice of you."

"*** I could suck *** it. Maybe no *** *** find me *** funny *** I find myself. Especially sponsors. I'd be out *** that money up front *** nothing."

"I'm pretty sure you don't have to worry about that."

"It's *** gamble. A big ***."

"Yeah." I bump my shoulder against his. "But honestly, you never know what you're capable of until you try. And this is a nice thing you're doing for your family. If you want, I can help you fundraise for the equipment. Mow lawns or have a car wash or something."

He looks at me, studying my face.

The minnows in my belly scurry. I turn away. "You'll have to work on the funny part, though."

He stands and yanks me toward the water. "*** that right?" For a second, I think he's going to splash me, but he stops—probably remembering my aids.

That doesn't mean I can't splash him. So I do.

He wipes water from his eyes and says, "I guess *** *** to watch *** see."

———

Mom hands Troy half of a leftover sub, and by the time we're done eating, his mom's there to get him. Instead of leaving, she hangs out with my parents while Colby and Troy head toward the water with the surfboards. Dad says he'll join us in a minute, and Mom's just happy to see us doing our thing. Before I go, I hand her my hearing aids and instantly the ringing in my ears grows louder. Troy's mom gives me a sorta-smile. Kind of like she feels bad for me. Hearing loss sure brings a lot of awkwardness with it.

On the sand, Troy knocks my board to the ground. "Last *** *** *** *** egg."

I stick out my leg to trip him, grab my board, and dart for the water. I beat him, though barely. The salt water sprays my face and rushes through my hair as I climb onto my board. It feels awesome, and I plan to make Mom and Dad promise not to wait so long to do this again. The waves are ankle biters, but they'll do.

The three of us wait for the swell, but both of them let me have it when we feel the water pull. I paddle hard. The wave sets up to be kind of decent. I hop to my feet, knees bent, and I'm stable for about two seconds. But suddenly the sun, the beach, and the clouds are spinning. I blink tightly and open my eyes wide, but I can't keep my balance.

Face first, I fall into the water. The wave gulps me, yanking my board away and dragging me with it. I'm not prepared for this and swallow at least a gallon of salt water.

Troy grabs me from above, and I'm grateful, because even though the waves are small, for a second, I couldn't tell which way was up. I cough up ocean juice and grab ahold of my board to keep afloat. I can't even imagine if the waves had been bigger.

"*** *** heck?" Colby says when he finally reaches me.

Mom and Dad are both in the water now too, and they're dragging me, on my board, toward shore. They, like me, have obviously made the connection to my ears.

One sucky thing about hearing loss and tinnitus is that they can totally mess with your equilibrium. And without equilibrium, it's pretty darn hard to balance on a surfboard. This past summer, I worked as a mother's helper watching a little girl every day, and I did notice that sometimes my balance was a tiny bit shaky. Even though I haven't had a chance to surf since last May, I probably should have guessed this would happen.

Mom rubs my back. "*** *** okay?"

"I'm fine." I shrug her hand off as I rip the board's leash from my ankle. But honestly, I feel like my heart's torn up. What if I can never surf again?

Troy and Colby follow us out of the water. Once Mom brings me my aids and stops fussing over me, she and Dad say they need to go for a walk. I watch Colby sprint toward the blanket and pick up his phone. It must have been ringing.

Troy sits next to me on the sand. I hold my breath to keep tears—which are pulling like the ocean's swell behind my eyeballs—from spilling. But when he puts his arm around me, I can't help myself any longer, and they fall like angry waves breaking.

Troy doesn't try to tell me lies—that everything will be fine. He just hands me a towel to wipe my snotty nose. He says, "I'll be *** Delphinus any time you need, Star Girl."

He's always teased me about my love of stars because I've grown up obsessing over the lore that goes with them. Troy knows Delphinus is my favorite, and for him to say this . . . well, it makes me cry even harder, and he just keeps on holding me.

———

Troy and his mom are gone, and Colby's near the water, still talking on his phone. As we clean up, Mom hugs me out of nowhere.

"I'm fine," I lie as I hug her back.

"Are *** sure?" Mom grabs my hand and looks me in the face. "Your dad and I have been talking for a while now. These little situations *** all adding up. We care about *** and want to see you get back to *** old routine. Back to when you *** happy and . . ."

She hesitates, so I say, "And what?"

"Honestly . . ." She looks to Dad for backup. "We feel like you've lost *** much of your confidence. *** cutting people out."

"I'm not cutting people out! I hang with Jenika all the time. And Troy too."

She goes on, "You *** get involved *** things anymore and—"

"Seriously? You're not making sense. I'm running for class president. Tomorrow. Doesn't that count?"

Dad says, "Of course *** does, and we *** so happy when you told us."

Mom gives Dad her *you-better-tell-her* look, and he exhales loudly. He turns to me. "We know you're trying to keep up *** sense of normalcy. And we also know *** secretly struggle to do so. All the time. Even here *** our conversation tonight."

I slap my knees. "Yes, but if you wouldn't mumble, I wouldn't struggle! I can't make my ears hear you, but you can change how you talk, so that I can hear. Seriously, you two should be making more of an effort than anyone."

Dad says clearly, "You're right. I'm sorry. Do you know how hard it is to see you like that, though? It literally breaks our hearts, Ray."

Mom's nodding.

"All this because I fell off my board?"

"You know it's more than that," Dad says. "Your mom and I have been discussing your hearing at great length. We've done research. Weighed the pros and cons of all the options. And I do mean *all* the options. Mom even joined a support group that Dr. Olsen told her about."

"For real? A support group?" Like Mom's the one with the problem. Sometimes I think she likes attention. When she's with her friends she's always blabbing personal stories, private ones. Especially about Colby and me. People eat it right up. I can't stand it. Neither can Colby.

She snaps, "It's a place to ask questions of people *** have *** through this. That's all. *** I don't like the way you're speaking to ***." She closes her eyes and takes a long breath. "We're honestly only trying to help ***."

"What do you mean by *help*? You stopped asking me what I want to do about my hearing a long time ago." My hands are flying. I'm on a roll. Finally telling my parents everything they never asked to hear. "You keep talking about the cochlear implants like they're the only option. But I don't want them, and you don't seem to care."

Dad says, "It's not that we don't care. But sometimes, as parents, we have to make decisions. Hard ones. You need to trust that we're doing all the research to make sure we do the right thing."

"See what I mean?" I shake my head. "You're still ignoring what I want. Everything I just said. You want me to let you make the biggest decision of my life for me. It's not fair! I want to find out about the stem cells that Dr. James mentioned."

"Rayne." Mom tries to use her calm voice, which actually makes it hard to understand her with the ocean noise. I focus extra hard on her lips, and she leans in, I guess paying attention to my body language for once. "You *have* told us how you feel about the implants. We've listened. *** for stem cells, I've researched it. I promise you. But *** need to understand that we *** more than you. We're thinking long-term *** risks. There's *** guarantee the stem cell research will pan out. And I don't want *** to be a guinea pig *** it. It'll be years before it's proven to work or not. Years before side effects might *** up. We can't take that risk. You'll fall too far behind in school. In life. So yes, cochlear implants *** *** best option, because the hearing aids aren't helping like they need to. I hope you'll come around to see that."

"I've done my research too," I say. "Cochlear implants are permanent. *Permanent!* I'll be stuck with some bionic lumps sticking out of my head. And my hearing won't actually be normal again—everyone will sound like robots. Plus, what if it doesn't work? That's happened, you know. You can't just take it back, because there's no going back."

No one replies.

I grab Dad's hands. "Please."

He swallows deeply, his whole head moving with the motion. "We're listening. I promise you. But I'd like you to listen too."

"No!" I pace. "You guys can't make me do the surgery."

Dad says, "At this stage, we only want you to go with us for an appointment with the surgeon. Dr. Olsen saw your audiogram this week and wants to meet you. Just listen to what he has to say. That's all. One meeting."

"Dr. Olsen is a surgeon? I thought he was just a cochlear doctor Mom called for some information."

"*** didn't want *** panic ***, honey," Mom says. "I *** you've *** sensitive about this . . ."

My heart squeezes itself. I'm definitely not going to see this surgeon. The only place I'm going is away from here. I take off down the beach, running until my breath is completely gone.

I climb an empty lifeguard shelter, hoping no one will find me. I lean against the smooth wooden wall before sliding down onto the platform floor. It's so unfair. I swear I hate my ears. My stupid aids. I rip them from my head and chuck them over the railing, hoping they'll get lost in the sand forever.

———

When I finally climb down, Colby's sitting against a nearby palm tree, obviously making sure I don't escape any farther.

Okay, so I know that's not true. I mean, it's Colby, not Mom or Dad. The sun is dipping behind the condos at the edge of the beach as I make my way over to him, and without a word, he hands me my aids.

There's not a speck of sand on them, not even in the air tube, so he must have spent a while cleaning them off. I put them in. "Thanks," I say, feeling extra awful that he's missing time with Sierra. "Sorry you had to wait for me."

"I didn't *** to do anything." He tosses his arm over my shoulder.

Mom and Dad are gone when we get back. I ask, "Where'd they go?"

"*** texted them that I *** *** *** and that I'd bring *** home. They *** good with that." He picks up the lone surfboard next to our bag. "Come ***," he says. "Give it another shot. Maybe that *** just a fluke earlier. I'm *** even going to get *** my board. I'll just stand *** *** water *** case *** need me, okay? I won't let anything happen. *** I think *** can *** this. *** *** just unprepared before."

Unprepared is right. But will I be able to balance better now that I know to be extra careful? I don't know what I'll do if I can never surf again, so maybe I should try. Alone with just Colby.

I stare out at the water. The waves are still pretty small. The choice is mine. All mine. Surf? Don't surf? Paddle or wait for the next wave? Something bigger. Better. Duck dive, or turtle, or ride the foam? Figuring out which way to paddle. Decisions made only by me.

Not Mom. Not Dad.

I turn to Colby, handing him my hearing aids while grabbing the board from under his arm. "Let's go." I'm cautious as I toss the board into the water and belly flop onto it. There's hardly a break, but

I paddle out to where the waves are catchable and tether the board to my ankle as I wait, gripping the board tightly with my knees so I don't flip over. I'm wobbly, but so far, so good.

The tide pulls me. Before I paddle, I close my eyes and smile at the last of the sunshine as it warms my face.

The board's nose lifts into the air. I go. The wave raises the back of my board, taking over. Instinctively, I pop up. My whole body braces to recalculate my center of balance, but once I'm fully standing, everything spins again. *Don't panic. Do not panic!*

And even though I don't, the whirling in my head is too much, sending me tumbling into the ocean.

I break through the surface, rip the leash from my ankle, and stand. I slap at the water over and over. Colby's racing to get to me, but I don't want his help. I don't need his help. I lift the board over my head and chuck it toward the horizon, hoping the waves will carry it out to sea forever, because I'm never going to need it again.

CHAPTER 4

I flop onto my bed and open my laptop, tears splashing onto the keyboard, which fits right in with the crashing waves on my screensaver. Both salty. Both angry.

Lucky tramples across the two dolphins on my comforter and snuggles under my arm. She licks my face as I wipe my cheeks, promising myself that I'll never let another I-feel-sorry-for-myself tear fall again.

My phone dings.

Jenika: *Ugh, volleyball sucked today.*

Jenika's got a no-drama policy, so if she says it was bad, it was bad.

Me: *???*

Jenika: *Can't stand Coach A. I swear I'm gonna quit.*

Me: *Nooo! You're the best on the team.*

Jenika: *Ugh, can't take him, Ray. How are you?*

Me: *. . . still deaf :/*

I send her an ear emoji.

Jenika: *Stop! You hear fine.*

Jenika moved here from Mississippi four years ago when her dad got a big promotion to vice president of sales for some fancy yacht company. She stood right in front of our third-grade class and introduced herself like she was running for student government president—trust me, I'd watched campaign speeches at Dad's school every year since I could remember, and Jenika was a pro. She stared each of us right in our faces and didn't mess up her words even once. I knew right then I wanted to be friends with her. Her public speaking talent hasn't necessarily rubbed off on me, but she's the queen of all things happy, and I appreciate that she's trying to make me feel better now.

Me: *Not according to my parents.*

Jenika: :(*Speech done for tomorrow's election?*

Me: *Yeah. BTW, Colby's home.*

Jenika: *Ohhhh be right over. Blame it on homework . . . you missed 6th hour.*

Because I'm now nearly deaf, Mom's making me meet with our school psychologist every other week. For someone who swears I'm falling behind in school, she doesn't seem to care that this makes me miss class.

Me: *Homework for real or an excuse to come drool over Colby?*

Jenika: *Both!* ☺ *Grady assigned a biography project. Details when I arrive.*

Me: *See you soon.*

I kept the brochure for Bayview School for the Deaf and Blind. For some reason, I can't stop thinking about it and wondering how the kids who go there feel. While I wait for Jenika, I grab the brochure and study the deaf side again, but it's hard to tell anything from the small pictures. I look it up online, but not the official boring site that will surely make the school seem like Disney World. Instead, I go to ChannelThis, because I want to see what real kids are posting about it. The truth.

I find a video of a boy who's a senior there. Luckily, there are captions, because I don't understand his sign language. He lives at the school during the week and is on the football team. How does someone play football if they can't hear?

As happy as he looks—he really does seem to love the school—it's obvious that I'd never fit in there myself. It's hard for me to communicate at school now; I'd never make it at Bayview without knowing sign language.

I jot his name in my notebook and write:

A) He's been there since he was little.

B) He's been deaf his whole life.

C) He signs, so it's easy for him.

Conclusion: It's not the place for me at all.

I close out of that tab and instead look up information about stem cells. The basic concept sounds pretty simple, but like Mom said, it doesn't seem like it'll happen in the next year or anything. I was hoping she was wrong about that.

Next, I type *cochlear implants*. When I click on the images, I'm bombarded with a bazillion photos of kids sporting high-tech ears with smiles plastered on their faces. The implants look as bad as I remember. Are the people in the photos just actors? Maybe they got paid to pretend they're happy having Frankenstein-like knobs coming out of their heads, because I can't believe the implants help enough that anyone would be *that* thrilled to have them. Right? How do you brush your hair? That has to hurt.

I flip over, staring at my favorite surfboard lights strung above my bed. I stand and yank them down, sending the thumbtacks flying and making Lucky leap. "Sorry, girl!" I pet her head and chuck the lights into my trashcan.

When I sit, Lucky snuggles up again, and I pull out my speech for the election. This girl, Sabrina, is running against me. Hopefully, no one who really cares about our school will vote for her. She's never once volunteered to help out before, so I'm not sure why she's running. The Harvest Drive's our most important charity event for the whole year, and it's coming up soon. I doubt Sabrina would stay after school for two weeks stuffing bags.

I hear Mom and Jenika outside my door before Lucky does—such a terrible watchdog. I stick my ear to the door and try to hear what they're saying, pushing the button on my right aid to raise the volume. But it's still too muffled.

When Jenika finally comes in, Lucky wags her tail wildly and circles Jenika's feet.

"Hey." She plops onto my orange saucer chair.

"Volleyball was bad?"

"That can wait. Your mom told me about your ears."

I swat the air. "No. Tell me what's wrong."

She shakes her head. "I don't understand Coach A.

All he does *** yell. It's not *** fun. Sports are supposed to be fun, right? Why *** play? I swear every one *** *** wants to quit." She takes a sip of her water.

"That sucks," I say. "I know it's not the Olympics, or even a high school team, but I hope you won't let him mess with your head. You're too good to quit."

"It's whatever, I ***." She sighs. "*** mom's hoping I'll convince you that *** implants *** cool."

"Right." I fluff a pillow and sit against it. "Did you get to see Colby when you came in?"

"Yeah, he looks awesome, *** always. But don't change *** subject on me. *** okay?"

"I'm good," I lie. But it's Jenika. And I need someone who will give me an objective opinion. Or at least listen to *my* opinion. "Okay, fine. I'm not good. I'm terrible. And I don't know what my mom told you, but my parents are being completely unreasonable!"

I spill the details about how I had to guess more than ever at Dr. James's on Monday, so in a way I'm worried that Mom's right. My hearing *might be* getting worse. I tell her about the beach and the surgeon. About how I ran away to the lifeguard station, but I wish I'd had the guts to run even farther. "Why am I always such a chicken?"

She's tapping the beads at the bottom of two of her braids together, looking down at them. "Maybe *** *** ***"

"Jenika," I snap, pointing to my ears.

"Sorry, sorry, sorry." She keeps her face toward mine, so I can read her lips. "I said, maybe there's another way."

"Like what?"

She tosses the braids over her shoulder. "I don't know. But there's got to be something."

"Maybe if I find convincing information about the stem cell stuff, my parents will listen."

"Is that what you really want?" Her head tilts.

"What do you mean?"

"I mean, do *** think that's what's going to make everything better *** you?"

"If my mom is going to make me do *something*, I'd pick stem cells over the cochlear thing a hundred times over. I looked it up. It's not surgery. And it's a fix that will make me hear like usual. Not robotic."

She looks me straight in the eye. "But what if your parents didn't make you pick? What if you could just be the way you are?"

I don't even know how to answer. My parents are great. But for as long as we've known about my hearing loss, they've been searching for a solution. A way to fix me—my brokenness. And I do feel broken. Or maybe just left out. And it seems like the only way I'll be able to communicate with my friends again is to fix my ears like Mom wants. But not *how* Mom wants.

"I just want to hang with everyone and understand whole conversations again. I'm pretty sure that requires A, better hearing aids, which aren't an option since I already have the newest and strongest ones out there; B, cochlear implants, which I refuse; or C, a stem cell transplant. Option three is seriously my only hope."

I glance at the Bayview brochure, but even that's no good because I'd be left out there too. I toss it on the floor.

Jenika asks, "Has *** mom even checked *** stem cell stuff out?"

"In her stack of papers, she only has one thing printed out about it, so she didn't look too hard. That's what makes me so mad." Maybe Mom would believe in it if I could find a doctor to tell her that it could happen. That it's coming soon. Then she'd agree to wait.

Jenika pushes me over on my bed, sits, and grabs my laptop. She taps the keys: *stem cells for hearing loss.* "Whoa!"

"What?" I look at the screen. There are a bazillion articles from schools like Stanford and Harvard about stem cell research trials specifically for hearing loss. I hadn't seen them before, maybe because I searched for stem cell research in general. I read the article from Harvard, which is all the way in Boston. "What do you think they mean by trials? And where's Stanford?"

Jenika looks it up. "California."

"Is there anything closer?"

"It doesn't need *** be close as long as *** have what *** need."

"I don't want to give my mom any reason to say no, so the closer the better."

"But *** Stanford's *** best, don't *** think *** parents would at least check it ***?"

"How do you know it's the best?"

"Sorry. I said if."

I take my laptop from Jenika and scroll, and scroll, and scroll. "It'll take me forever to read all these sites and figure out which university is the best to contact."

At the bottom of the second page, I click a link for The National Institute on Deafness and Other Communication Disorders (NIDCD). I skim through the information on their site. Even though it's located in Maryland, it sounds like it's a place that keeps track of research from all over.

Jenika says, "I bet someone *** can help *** figure out what *** ***. It's like *** specialty."

She's probably right, and a little piece of hope warms my whole body. I type an email and can't hit send fast enough. Please, please answer quickly. Like before morning. So I don't have to have the same old discussion with Mom at breakfast. I'm tired of being the one doing all the listening.

CHAPTER 5

Even though my boomingly-loud alarm clock is set to go off in the morning, Mom doesn't trust it. She taps my arm five minutes before I need to be up.

"Moooom," I moan as I sit up and put in my aids. My notebook's open on the nightstand. The words *Stanford, Harvard, and NIDCD (Maryland)* are extra dark—traced over a million times. I reach for it super casually and flip it closed, then spring out of bed to load my backpack before getting dressed. Thankfully, it seems Mom hasn't caught sight of my notebook page. No need to argue over trials before I've got some real information.

She kisses my head and hands me a plate with a piece of homemade crumb cake—my favorite— before leaving my room. "I'll *** *** *** library *** *** you. *** *** get nervous, just *** my ***."

Seriously, how does she expect me to hear her

when she's walking away? I can pretty much guess what she said, though. And I appreciate her trying, but I'm still mad at her. If I do get nervous—which I won't because even though I hate people looking at me, I've done this before, and I've practiced my speech a thousand times—I'll be sure to look at Jenika.

Dad comes in next holding my favorite shirt, which he obviously ironed for me.

"Aren't you going to be late for work?" I ask.

"Couldn't leave without telling *** how proud of *** I am. Knock 'em dead, sweetheart."

"Thanks." I hug him. "That's the plan."

With both of them finally gone, I check my email. "Please, please, please let there be an answer," I say through a mouthful of crumb cake. But my inbox is empty.

———

On my way to Jenika's, I text her.

Me: *OMG, OMG, OMG . . . Did you see R-Jarrow's Snap&Share?*

Jenika: *YES! Was just texting you. What's it mean?*

Me: *A clue! New album release??? 9 rings and pink lights. 9? OMG, been so long.*

Jenika: *9th of this month? That's a Friday. Makes sense. If so, only a week away!*

Me: *Need to figure out the clues. Must stay up and hear it as soon as it drops!!!!!*

She doesn't answer.

Me: *Hello????*

Two minutes later, Jenika's walking toward me, quickly. In the opposite direction of school. She spins me around. "Let's figure out this R-Jarrow thing."

"Okay, but let's do it on the way to school." I try to turn us back around.

She isn't budging.

I yank my arm from her grip. Behind her, I see Troy walking toward school with some girl, and they're both laughing. I squint to make sure I'm seeing clearly.

"Sorry," Jenika says.

"Is that Lourdes?"

She nods. "She was waiting *** him when he passed *** house."

Okay. Yeah. I have to focus on the election, but I'm already in a rotten mood about everything that happened with my parents yesterday and the fact that my email inbox was empty this morning. So Troy—well, maybe he's just been extra nice because of my ears. Maybe he likes someone else. My stomach sinks.

"Hello." Jenika waves her hand in my face. "Are *** listening to me?"

I nod.

"We don't need *** to throw *** *** *** *** ***. *** focus."

I tune her out as my mind wanders all over the globe. Suddenly, I have an urge to cut school. I could catch the city bus and be at the beach in less than twenty minutes. I mean, I've never ridden the public bus before, and I've never skipped school before either, but today seems like a good day to try both.

Jenika snaps her fingers. "What is wrong *** ***?"

"Yeah, it's whatever," I say. "Let's just get out of here. We can go to the beach." I turn toward the east and raise my face to the warm sun that's rising overhead like a loyal friend.

"*** *** serious, Rayne?" She yanks me, so I'm facing her. "You'd never *** it."

I'd never do it if I were alone, because I picture a grumpy old guy who would mumble all his words while giving me directions, and I know I wouldn't be able to understand a single word of it. Even if I were to ask a simple question like, *Is this the bus to Pompano Beach?* I'd probably confuse yes for no, or no for yes. It's just the way my ears mix up sounds, like a blender, constantly whirling consonants and vowels around inside my head while I try to puzzle them together correctly. Without a shake or a nod, yes and no are easily jumbled, and sometimes I feel like nearly deaf equals stupid.

I pull my arm free. "I would so! Come on." For once, I'm going to be spontaneous. I'm going to break Mom's rule. And the school's rule. I'm going to the beach! Sabrina can be president. I don't even care anymore.

I take four steps, my pace quickening with my heartbeat. Jenika falls in next to me with a big ol' smile on her face, the beads on the tips of her braids *click-click-click*ing to match our strides. On the fifth step, I realize I have no money to pay the bus fare. I realize I don't even know where the closest bus stop is. I don't have my sunscreen. Or a hat. Or a ponytail holder. Jenika can't miss volleyball, or she'll be benched. On the eighth step, I stop.

I turn around. "Or maybe we ought to just go to school."

"Yeah, probably ***." Jenika loops her arm in mine, not even once saying I-told-you-so, though I do hate that she's always right about me. I'm a big scaredy-cat. When I get home, I'll be sure to check bus routes and prices, so next time I can be prepared to actually be spontaneous and skip school.

Like she knows I'm stuck inside my head, Jenika changes the subject. "Did *** have *** email when *** woke up? We going to California for *** miracle?"

"No, not yet." I'm glad to have a best friend who doesn't care that I have a hearing problem, who isn't embarrassed to be seen with me, and who even offered to learn sign language with me if my ears ever get that bad. And now she's willing to go to California with me? I love her!

But as much as she tells me I shouldn't be embarrassed about my hearing, I can't help wondering if she'd feel different about all this if *she* were the one going deaf. I wonder if she'd really have picked the hot pink, over-the-ear hearing aids she tried to convince me to get—rather than the skin-tone ones I ended up with because hopefully they'd be a whole lot less noticeable. Shame's easy to avoid when you're not the one with the problem.

The hallways of Sea Ridge Middle School are super loud. Dr. James says I should try to avoid loud places because they could damage my ears more, but it's not like I can just skip school every day.

Even with Jenika walking next to me, I can't really understand anything she's saying—the background noise is too much. She stops to talk with our usual group of friends near the media center, and even though Troy is there, I pretend I don't notice any of them and keep walking because there are two things I know for sure:

A) When you can't hear well, it's exhausting to focus on words, and I need to save all my energy for the speeches later.

B) Since we're later than usual, the bell is about to ring, and to me, its sound is piercing and makes my hearing aids echo for seconds after the actual bell stops. Anyone nearby can hear the lingering feedback shooting from my head, like a microphone screeching because it's too close to the speaker. Most of the time, people are confused, trying to figure out where the sound's coming from, but word's getting around that it's me and my bionic ears. If only it were a superpower.

Luckily, I scoot into homeroom before the bell blares. Troy tugs on my arm just inside the door.

"*** a hurry?" he asks.

Kids are pouring in, and it's really loud.

"Me?" My stomach's prickly inside. "No. Well, yes." I stop. "I didn't finish my homework." It's not a lie. I fell asleep as soon as Jenika left last night.

"*** last two *** *** *** the appendix, not *** ***."

Wait, what? "Something's wrong with your appendix?"

Kids turn to look at Troy. One asks, "You okay, bro?"

"Fine, yeah." He waves them off and pulls me aside. "I said, the last two answers are in the appendix, not the chapter."

"Right." My cheeks burn. "Thanks for the tip."

I pass Jenika's empty desk near the back of the room and want so badly to plop into it. If she came in and saw me, she wouldn't even blink. She'd go right to the front of the room and sit in my spot. But Mr. Walsh would eventually notice and make a big deal about it. That would be worse than taking my usual seat to begin with. So I keep walking, front and center.

Because Mom made such a huge deal about my bad ears last year, I now have my very own IEP. She told me to think of it as an I'm-Especially-Privileged document, rather than the Individualized Education Plan that it actually is. You know, the same thing all the "exceptional education" kids have. But there's definitely no privilege in having to sit right up front in every single class. And maybe the kids who have been exceptional all their lives don't mind, but it's a whole other story when you become exceptional so suddenly.

Beth, a girl in my usual group of friends, crouches next to my desk so we're eye level, and her face is close to mine. "Rayne, I looked *** you before class to give you ***, but you hardly hang out *** *** halls this year." She hands me an envelope. "I'm having *** pool party *** my birthday next weekend. I hope *** come."

"Oh, um, thanks." I rip open the seal and look at the awesome handmade invite—Beth wants to be an artist someday, and I guarantee she'll be super successful. The party's a week from Sunday, but as soon as she said *pool*, it was a no for me. "Darn! I'm so sorry," I lie. "It's my grandmother's birthday. We have a family thing." My stomach sinks as her face falls. I hate this, but a pool party means I'll sit by myself on a lounge chair while everyone else has chicken fights because, for me, going in the water would mean taking out my aids, and without them, I'm mostly deaf. Another lose-lose situation for me.

"Bummer. Well, it starts pretty early, *** my parents said people could stay till *** seven, *** maybe *** *** *** before *** after *** grandmother's birthday thing."

I shake my head. "No." *Think, think, think.* "Um, we're taking her to her favorite restaurant near Key Largo. It's going to be an all-day thing."

"Okay. ***, maybe *** can sleep over *** night ***. We haven't talked *** *** while." She stands.

This is awful. I'm awful. I'm the worst friend ever. "Yeah. We should try to set something up." Maybe. Maybe not. I mean, I guess doing something with just the two of us would make it easier to hear. I should make a plan with her. Like now. But I can't bring myself to do it.

"Cool. *** talk later." Beth walks to her desk.

Mr. Walsh wanders the room collecting our homework while he lectures about Newton's first law of motion. I love science, and this year we'll be studying lunar tides and the properties of waves—which I cannot wait for—but this part is a snooze.

Mr. Walsh has his back to me as he collects homework from the kids in the last row. "Newt*** Law *** states *** object *** *** stay at *** *** ***."

He heads toward the front. "So *** essence, if nothing *** happening to you, and nothing does happen, you'll never go anywhere." I wonder how this Newton guy gets credit for being a genius when this seems pretty obvious to me. Mr. Walsh reaches out his hand for my homework and says, "Rayne, where's *** device thing *** me? *** mom emailed *** teachers to make *** we're using it."

She what? I nearly choke on spit that's entered the wrong pipe in my throat. Maybe no one heard that. Maybe it wasn't as loud as it seemed to me—which is a ridiculous thought, given my ears. Sure enough, everyone's staring. Waiting to see what I'll do.

What I want to do is vanish. Escape. Be rescued by Delphinus.

I twist toward the front. "Um, Mr. Walsh, it's okay," I practically whisper. "I can actually hear you fine." It's not a lie. The classroom isn't huge, and as long as everyone's quiet while he's talking, and as long as I can see his face, I never really have a problem. And the few times I do, that's what the volume button on my aids is for.

"Sorry. Rules *** rules." He continues collecting papers from everyone, but when he gets to the front, he stands over me, and I'm forced to dig through my backpack and hand over the SurfCon remote. As if calling a Bluetooth microphone device something that cool would fool anyone. I slipped it to Mr. Walsh once last month before anyone got to class. Sure, it worked—transmitting Mr. Walsh's voice directly into my aids—but everyone talked for days about his weird necklace. I never offered it up again. I'm so sick of Mom butting in.

As Mr. Walsh slips the cord over his head and around his neck, I sink into my seat and doodle Delphinus. Save me!

CHAPTER 6

All day I practice my speech in my head. I can't even focus in class. I'm so ready for this, and I know I'm the right person for the job, but lately things don't seem to be going my way.

Jenika waves her hand in my face in the hallway near the library. "Hello, *** talking to ***."

"What if I tank this?" I lean against a door, thinking it's closed, and end up falling on my butt inside the custodian's storage room.

Mr. Faro helps me up. "*** okay, Rayne?"

I've known Mr. Faro since I was little, and even though he's super nice, he's quiet. In the summers, when I help my mom get her classroom ready, Mr. Faro is always working hard and always has a smile on his face, but I've only heard him speak a few times.

"Yes, sorry," I say. "I didn't realize the door was cracked."

"No problem." He walks me out. "Good luck *** there, *** afternoon. You've got ***."

"Thank you." I guess he's seen the campaign posters all over the hallways.

Jenika walks with me to the library and straightens my shoulders. "*** were born *** this. No worrying. Just do *** thing."

"Right."

She adds, "If any*** can lead the school, it's ***. And everyone knows it. Plus, *** got votes from *** whole volleyball team. This will be *** sweat!"

"Thanks." I definitely appreciate her pep talk. The school needs someone who can raise spirit. Someone who can convince kids that it isn't dorky to wear their school colors proudly and to actually dress up for spirit days. That's me, for sure. At least it used to be. Lately, I seem to doubt so many things.

Mom's standing in the back and gives me a thumbs-up. Everyone in the room knows I did a great job as president last year, so I hope they'll all truly vote for the most qualified candidate.

Sabrina goes first and her speech is awful. She didn't write a single thing down and doesn't talk at all about what she wants to accomplish. I have no clue why she didn't prepare for this. I actually feel a little bit bad for her.

When it's my turn, I nail my speech. I barely read from the notecards, so I'm able to look around the room and read people's faces while I talk. Eye contact is everything. I think they like my ideas. I'm sure people can tell I want to make school more fun.

I take my seat next to Sabrina, and Mom blows me a kiss on her way out. She mouths, *Great job*, and I smile.

Mr. Grady goes to the podium. "Thank ***, girls. I'd like to invite *** *** back up ***. *** going to open *** *** to questions."

I forgot about this part, but I've got a definite advantage with all my experience from last year.

The first question is for Sabrina. Tracy asks her where she got her adorable skirt. For real. I'm suddenly nervous that Sabrina could win.

Jenika rolls her eyes.

The second question comes from a kid named Quinton all the way in the back of the room. I hear him say my name, but after that, it's all jumbled. Seriously, I can't hear him. I scramble toward him, sticking my head out as far as it'll go, trying to catch his words. *Focus on his lips.*

"What *** *** plan to *** *** ***, *** *** get elected? *** *** terrible."

I'm midway across the room when he's done, so I stop and let my heart slow. I'm pretty sure of what he said. And it sounds like something Quinton would ask, so I answer, "That's an easy one. Some more things we can do are to add pep rallies, dodgeball tournaments, and even a field day. Why let the elementary kids have all the fun?" I wait for everyone to clap; after all, my ideas mean getting them out of class. A lot.

Instead, the room is dead silent.

Do they hate my answer? That's not possible. Which means I must've have gotten the question totally wrong.

While I'm trying again to piece together the words I heard and fill in the ones I didn't, this kid Adam says, "Okay ***. I guess we can try *** eat a dodgeball. Maybe *** consider it *** delicacy?"

The entire room cracks up. I have no idea what to do. Say something? Laugh with them? Pretend I did it on purpose? I'm getting used to pulling tricks.

I blink, hard and fast, trying to catch my breath.

I say, "Um, I have to use the bathroom. Sorry."

And I run.

People laugh even harder as I slip out the door.

Heat stings behind my eyes. I don't know where to go. The door to the custodian's storage room is still open, so I slip inside and close it.

I shove a metal rack, and rolls of toilet paper scatter to the ground. As soon as Mr. Grady said there'd be questions, I should've known I'd have trouble. These awful hearing aids are pointless.

Mr. Faro comes in. "Goodness." He lifts my face. "What's ***? Let me get *** mom."

"No." I grab his arm. "Please don't. I'm sorry. I'll leave."

"*** can't go leaving like ***." He hands me a tissue from one of the cabinets and pushes the door open all the way. "What's got *** *** upset?"

I hope no one I know walks by. "I'm pretty sure I bombed the election."

He sits on the edge of his desk. "Why do *** *** that?"

I wipe my cheeks. "Do you ever wish you could be invisible?"

"Well . . ." He crosses his arms over his chest. "*** can't get more invisible *** my job."

"What do you mean?"

"I'm *** shadow around here, at least *** someone needs something."

That's actually really sad. "Yeah, but if people don't notice you, then they can't laugh at you either."

He leans forward. "Is that why you want to be invisible?"

"Sort of." I wish I could come to school and be left alone. I'd do my work, go home, watch movies, play with Lucky. I'd be fine. Or I could take classes online, if they used closed captions. Then I wouldn't have to sit up front. Or hand over my SurfCon. "It's just . . ." I pick at a thread in my jean shorts. "I feel stuck all the time lately. My head is mixed up. Sometimes I want to be invisible. But sometimes I wish I could just be the me I was two years ago." Or even just one year ago, when my ears were still mostly fine.

"Why *** that?"

I hesitate. I don't know Mr. Faro that well. Still, he's always been nice. I have a feeling I can trust him with the thoughts slamming through my head. "Because that me could hear. That me wasn't fighting with her parents or worried that she's missing out on things all day long. That me wasn't scared of anything." I add, "Back then, I liked me." I lean against the cold wall. My words surprise me. All the things I've been feeling are right there in the open. And they're all true, but I still can't believe I'm telling them to him. I wish the day would be over already.

"*** need to let go *** *** brake."

"What?"

"*** like *** bike ride?"

I nod.

"It's great, especially *** *** ocean path, right?"

I nod again.

"But it's not nearly *** fun when *** have to pump *** brakes all *** time. Let go *** *** brake, and enjoy *** ride. Seems like *** only one stopping *** is yourself."

Is that true? Or are Mom and Dad stopping me? I'm not sure. Probably both. But if I'm riding the bike, I should be the one in control of my own brakes.

CHAPTER 7

Jenika texts me after school saying she looked everywhere but couldn't find me before she had to go to practice. Guess the custodian's room is a good hideout.

I wait a few hours to answer her, not just because she's at practice but also because I don't feel like talking, and she has a way of dragging things out of me. But even though I've tried all afternoon to forget the election disaster, I have to know.

Me: *Hey. Hope practice was good. What did Quinton ask today during my speech?*

Jenika: *Hi! You okay? I can't believe Adam was so rude to you at the Q&A. But I promise nobody was paying attention to him. Come sleep over? We can talk more in person. I have ice cream!*

I'm most definitely not in the mood for a sleepover. Even at Jenika's. There are some things she'll never be able to fix.

Me: *Not tonight. Colby's still home. Quinton's question???*

Jenika: *He asked what you plan to do about the cafeteria food.*

Seriously?

But for real, food . . . fun. They sound a lot alike. Anyone could have gotten confused.

Me: *Oh, right. Thanks.*

She texts me that the election went on as planned, by secret ballot, and we'll find out the results Tuesday morning, since Monday's a holiday. Mr. Faro's right. Time to let go of the brakes.

———

Colby's going out with Sierra for her birthday, and Mom and Dad are going to the Sawgrass football game. I'm glad to be alone with Lucky. Time to do more research.

I pray extra hard before I open my email. *Hey there, Big Guy. I'd be really happy if you could help me out and make the email be there. Even better if it's good news. Thanks. Love, Me.*

Yes!

Dear Rayne,

Hello and thank you for reaching out to
the National Institute on Deafness and
Other Communication Disorders (NIDCD)
Information Center. We appreciate your
request for more information regarding
sensorineural hearing loss. The NIDCD
supports and conducts research and
training on normal and disordered
processes of hearing, balance, taste,
smell, voice, speech, and language.
We also develop and disseminate
health information based on scientific
discovery to the public.

You asked for information on stem cell
regeneration as it pertains to hearing
loss. Here are links to several
ongoing studies regarding this. In
addition, we have a web page listing
multiple ongoing clinical trials. We
hope you will browse them and see if
you are a candidate to participate in
one or more . . .

This is perfect. Better than I could have hoped for!

The email and all of the links are super scientific, so I spend the next few hours decoding what I can and logging everything in my notebook. No doubt, I'd make a great detective. The best part of it all is that there's actually a stem cell study going on in Orlando. Three hours away. So close!

And I meet all the criteria. Except that they want kids up to age ten. I'm sure if Mom called and worked her magic, they'd make an exception. I'm not all that much past ten anyway. And age shouldn't have anything to do with it. Hearing loss is hearing loss.

Best of all, though, it's not surgery, and it's not permanent. If it doesn't work, it's not like I'll lose what hearing I still have left. That almost always happens with implant surgery. This seems like a much better thing to try first.

I print the information and wait for the perfect time to bring it up. I'm confident that Mom and I may finally agree on something.

———

I check Snap&Share before I even get out of bed in the morning. On R-Jarrow's page, there's a photo of thirteen pastel-colored popcorn bags. Yes! But definitely not a countdown. Nine and thirteen? Maybe a date? September thirteenth is only ten days away. Ahhh!

I'm extra helpful making lunch, and for once, I actually want my parents to bring up my hearing problem, but they don't, probably because they're asking Colby a zillion questions about school while we eat.

Mom stirs her iced tea. "Why haven't *** *** us *** summer grades? They *** to be *** by ***."

"*** would think ***, but *** haven't posted yet." Colby piles up dishes and tries to make a break for the kitchen.

Mom pats the table, signaling Colby to sit. "I called *** registrar's office. *** said grades came out *** week after summer classes ended."

Oh, man. He's so busted.

Colby sits. "*** did?"

Dad shakes his head. "Come ***, son, we weren't born yesterday. And *** know *** rules. Good grades *** *** come home and go to BC."

Colby smiles. "Define *good*."

I laugh, because even though he's caught, Colby's still hilarious. And because my plan is to keep Mom and Dad in a decent mood, so I can spring the stem cell stuff on them.

But they don't laugh. They don't even smile.

Colby sighs. "Look, school's never *** easy *** me. *** know that. I got lucky *** had good grades anyway, but college *** hard. *** have to actually study. A lot. Like all *** time. I *** lucky *** get straight Cs!"

Part of me expects Mom to offer to move to Tampa so she can use her beachnics to bribe Colby to do his homework again. Part of me even wants her to. My hearing stuff would be so much easier to deal with if just Dad were here with me.

Mom's face is pink. She opens her mouth, but Dad touches her arm to stop her. He says, "College *** about growing up. *** have to be able to do this on *** own. Time management *** key. We'll give you another semester to figure it out, but at that point, if it's not As and Bs—I'll even allow one C—*** have to come home."

Colby's face is tight. "May I be excused?"

Mom says, "Help *** sister *** *** dishes first, please."

I stand and grab the stack Colby already piled. "It's okay. I've got it. You should go see Sierra while you can."

He looks at Mom and Dad, and both of them nod. He gives me a quick hug. "Thanks."

———

While I clean the kitchen, Mom's mumbling words, but the only ones I hear are *parenting, hard,* and *tired.* I can guess the context of it all, no problem.

Dad's extra loud when he says, "Someday you'll miss them when they're gone."

I peek above the countertop, hoping to stay covert, but Dad gives me a wink.

Mom's eyes are sad.

I grab her hand. "I'm not gone yet, so you should soak up every minute with me that you can. And I've been thinking, we should go get ice cream. You know, live it up."

Dad says, "That actually sounds great. It's a perfect day *** a bike ride."

Thankfully, I don't have to take my aids out to ride a bike, or else just like surfing, I might not be able to do that anymore either.

"Count me in," Mom says.

We park our bikes outside Cherry Smash, the cutest old-fashioned ice cream shop ever. It's the perfect location to talk about signing me up for this trial in Orlando. I'm hoping they'll be as happy about this opportunity as I am. We could have our bags packed and be on the road in less than an hour.

The smell of sugar rushes over me as soon as we walk in. Unfortunately, the loudness hits me too. I take out my phone and use the Bluetooth hearing aid app to change the setting to one that cuts out most of the background noise and is supposed to make it easier to hear people talking to me.

"*** Mr. Campbell!" one girl in a group of three calls from across the ice cream parlor, super loud. They're all wearing SHS shirts.

Of course, Dad goes over to talk with them while Mom and I wait in line. Mom jokes that Dad's like the mayor around here. Everyone knows him, and most everyone likes him. As cool as that is, sometimes, on days like this, when we have important things to discuss, I wish no one in town knew who he was. Except for the girl who finally rings us up, because she happens to be one of his students too, and she gives us her employee discount, which makes Mom happy. Which is really good for me.

I insist on a table snuggled deep in a corner nook that's about as private as we can get in the jam-packed shop and as far away from the jukebox as possible. I'm next to Dad and across from Mom. We settle into our sundaes, which are smothered in hot fudge and whipped cream—happiness in a bowl. After a few bites, I reach into my shorts pocket. My fingers shake as I unfold the printouts I've brought.

Mom stuffs an overflowing spoonful of gooey goodness in her mouth and mumbles, "What's ***?" She reaches for the papers.

Okay, so maybe the fudge sauce wasn't such a good idea, seeing how it's suddenly churning in my stomach. I need full confidence, so I straighten and clear my throat. "You and Dad are so busy, and I wanted to make your jobs easier. I know you stress a lot about my ears, so I did some research on my own for all of us."

Dad's eyebrows inch skyward, and he nods once, almost like he's impressed. I take it as a vote of confidence.

Mom's silent, inspecting every inch of the printouts, and I'm happy she's actually reading them.

I take the papers from her hand and flip to the third page. "I remember you saying once how you saved my umbilical cord when I was born."

Her face and Dad's both squish up, like they can't

hear me—which is a problem when I use this setting on my aids. I feel like I'm shouting, but I'm obviously not talking loudly at all.

I clear my throat and lean in. "You saved my umbilical cord, in case we ever needed it. Remember?" I point to the paper. "See here? This study is in Orlando, and they do an umbilical cord infusion back into my body so my own ear hairs might be able to fix themselves."

She doesn't say anything while her eyeballs scan the paper. Before I know it, she's shaking her head. "*** too old *** *** study."

"I know it says that, but you could call Dr. Brandt, the one in charge, and tell her about my situation. She'd probably let me in anyway. I mean, why not? What does age have to do with it anyway?"

Dad opens his mouth, but before he can speak Mom enunciates, "Sweetie, the world doesn't work that way. It just . . . doesn't."

I want so badly to blurt that the world *does* work that way. For Mom it always has. But I say nothing.

Dad pats her hand.

The tinkling bell on the front door echoes in my aids and lingers even after the tiny metal ball actually stops moving, teasing me with its cheerfulness.

Dad scoots closer, draping his arm over my shoulder and pulling me into his chest. It feels nice, and I can't remember the last time I felt so . . . I don't know, important? Safe? That's not quite right, but it's good. So good.

"Mom and I will talk about it."

"For real?" I pull away from him and inspect his face. Dad's eyes are like swimming pools of niceness, always sparkling, even when he has to tell people things they don't want to hear. He has a way about him like that. Honest. Kind. Kindly honest. So I know he's serious, because he wouldn't say it otherwise. I bury my head in his chest, and his arms envelop me, but that sets off the squealing of my aids again, and both of us flinch.

"Sorry!" he says. "I know you hate the attention that brings."

I hope he means the screeching and not the hug, because I don't hate his hugs. "It's okay."

"Seriously, ***, we'll talk about it. This *** at least worth asking about."

Mom nods.

"Thank you, thank you, thank you." I stand and hug Dad again, this time with my head above his shoulder, so as not to set my aids a-screeching.

I kiss Mom's cheek so she doesn't feel left out of my gratitude, even though Dad's the one who's actually considering the information. I sit again to finish my cherry-chunk ice cream sundae, but it's not easy with all the smiling my face is doing.

———

At home, Mom and Dad sit on the back patio. They say they have some talking to do. I hope Mom isn't going to try to talk Dad out of investigating the stem cell trial.

I take Lucky for a walk, but it doesn't keep my mind off what they're discussing, so I head to my room and turn on R-Jarrow. I love every song she's ever written, but I can hardly stand the wait for her new album. I really hope she's not tricking us with her posts.

My notebook's open to the page where Jenika and I listed the boys in our class in order of who's coolest. Troy Wolf was the top of the list for me, but I'd never tell him. I flip to a blank page and write a new list of names—people I can pick for my biography project. Mr. Grady says we can do anyone alive or dead.

Abigail Adams: not afraid to stick up for herself and what she believed in

R-Jarrow: best singer ever and does a ton of charity stuff

Martin Luther King, Jr.: one of the greatest speakers I've ever heard, not to mention a kick-butt activist

Jenika: the whole world needs to know this girl

I know Jenika would never be on board, though. She thinks I should do Helen Keller. To show everyone that I'm okay with who I am. But the truth is, I'm not really okay with it. And I'm not even sure why. I mean, I want to be okay. But everything feels off. So . . . new. And I don't know how to process the newness of it all.

Whenever I've heard people mention Helen Keller, they've talked about her like she was super saintly. But the book Jenika gave me says Helen Keller was an "unruly child" who threw a lot of temper tantrums. Sounds like a brat. We may both have hearing trouble, but I'm obviously nothing like her; I'm handling this like an adult.

I toss the book aside. I don't really see the point of biographies. It's not like reading a bunch of facts about Helen Keller would help anyone truly understand her—or me. I know this for sure, because even my own mom can't understand me. No, scratch that. *Can't* and *won't* aren't the same thing at all.

CHAPTER 8

"*** *** *** *** ***." Mom jiggles my shoulder, and Lucky licks my face.

I flip over, grab my aids, and pop them in.

"*** going *** early today, get dressed *** ask Jenika *** she wants *** to pick *** up on the way."

I rub the sleep from my eyes and scratch Lucky's ears. "What for?"

"It's *** surprise. Get moving." She closes my door when she leaves.

What are the chances the surprise involves Dr. Brandt's clinical trial? Maybe Mom's using school as a cover, and she's really taking Jenika and me to Orlando!

In an instant, I'm wide awake and moving as fast as possible. I pack an overnight bag too, just in case, and kiss Lucky on the head. "Hopefully, the next time I see you, I'll have good news."

I keep waiting for Mom to head toward the highway, and when we arrive at school, my body burns with disappointment.

Jenika mouths to me, *What's wrong?*

I shake my head.

Mom leads Jenika and me to the cafeteria kitchen. Ms. Belmont, the cafe manager, has been making me treats since I was a kid.

"Hello," Mom calls.

Suddenly there's a loud thud. Tomato sauce comes flying from behind a wall.

"*** ***." cries a voice.

We peek around the corner. The new cafeteria helper—I think her name is Ms. Timmes—has spilled a whole bag of chicken nuggets.

Her hand's over her heart, and she squeaks to Ms. Belmont, "Sorry. *** startled me. I tried to catch *** bag, but I knocked over *** red sauce instead."

"*** okay," Ms. Belmont says. "I'll text Mr. Faro to *** help *** clean it ***."

"We can help too," I say.

"Nope. Not today, ***." Ms. Belmont reaches for a plate on a top shelf and hands it to me. The cupcake is huge, decorated with purple frosting and colored sprinkles. "Today's *** day."

"But it's not my birthday."

Jenika practically yells, "Do *** know something we don't know, but something we want to know? Something *** hoping for?"

I'm so lost.

Mom's smiling, and Ms. Belmont's nodding wildly.

"Oh my gosh!" Jenika says. "Congratulations, Ray! *** did it!"

It takes me a second, but it finally sinks in. "I won?"

Mom hugs me. "I'm *** proud *** ***, Madam President."

I whisper, "Thank you." I want to be happy. I really do. Especially since I thought I might lose after the disaster on Friday. But I'm not. The only win I was hoping for today was for Mom to take me to Orlando.

Mr. Faro comes in with his mop and bucket and quietly goes right toward the spill. He really is a perfect shadow.

Before he can dip the mop, I go over to him. "Hi."

He faces me straight on—I'm guessing so I can see his lips. "Good morning. Did you ride this weekend? And loosen the brakes?"

"Well, I won the election. Maybe that counts?"

He does a funny wiggle dance. "I knew it. They *** a good leader *** they see one. I'm happy *** you."

I try not to laugh, but his dance is so funny that I can't help myself. Besides, I *did* win. People voted for me even though I messed up that question. That's worth celebrating! And even though I'm not headed to Orlando today, that doesn't mean I won't be soon.

Though I've never done it before, in that moment, I reach out and give Mr. Faro a giant hug. And he hugs me back.

When I pull away, he looks at me and reaches his arm out. His hand's not exactly a fist; instead, his thumb and the two fingers next to it point straight out. He double taps them while shaking his head no. I get that. He holds his palm straight up in the air and swooshes it down.

I shrug. "I don't know sign language."

"That's the sign for brake. So . . ." He does both signs again. "No brakes. I *** thinking over *** weekend: maybe sign language will help you let go."

Would it? "Thanks," I say as he grabs his mop from the bucket and gets to work. "Wait, how do I sign that?"

"I don't know. But when you learn, teach me."

On our way to class, Jenika pulls up R-Jarrow's Snap&Share account. We squeal when we see seven pink cotton candy cones. This is really happening.

I grab her arm. "Nine was definitely the month, and thirteen was the date. This next clue has to be the start of a countdown. September thirteenth is seven days away. That has to be it."

Jenika's jumping up and down. "One week. Just one. We *** last that long."

"I don't know," I say. "It's torture."

She holds the door open for me. "*** title *** going to have *** word pink *** it, I *** it. Or maybe *** cover will be pink. *** these photos have that going ***."

"Yeah, but a Tuesday is a weird day. Maybe it's just a song and not her whole album."

"Bite *** tongue." Jenika shoves me lightly. "When *** R-Jarrow ever followed *** protocol?"

"True." I drop my SurfCon on Mr. Walsh's podium and sit at my desk just as the announcements come on. Mr. Grady names the winners of the sixth-grade election first. When he gets to us, I stare straight ahead.

Mr. Grady says, "Congratulations *** Rayne Campbell, president *** *** grade."

Our whole class whoops and cheers. No lie.

Someone puts their arm around me from behind and says right into my hearing aid, "***. I *** *** ***."

I may have trouble hearing, but I know Troy's voice well.

I turn around, and he gives me a full-on hug. "Great job. I wanted to *** *** that *** other day, but I couldn't find ***. *** speech *** perfect. Did *** get my text?"

I did, but I didn't feel like talking to anyone right after the fiasco with the Q&A, and then I got so busy researching stuff over the weekend that I forgot to respond to Troy. "Yeah—sorry I didn't answer. I was spending time with Colby before he went back to school." It's a half-truth, anyway.

Mr. Walsh calls us all to attention, and I take one quick peek at Jenika.

She mouths, *I told you so!*

She did. And she was right. I'm president of the whole seventh grade.

———

There's no wasting time since the Harvest Drive and Fest is only two months away. We have our first student government meeting after school on Wednesday. This year, Mom's the sixth-grade sponsor, so she'll be here too, though I guess she's running late.

Sabrina walks in and sits next to me. She sounds excited when she says, "Hi. Congrats again. If it's okay, Mr. Grady said I can still volunteer."

I shrug. "Yeah, of course. I didn't think you were really interested in this, though."

"I ran, didn't I?" She opens her notebook. "Seems like SGA is a lot of fun, and I get bored at home, so here I am."

"Cool. And yeah, it's a lot of fun." She seems genuine about it, so it's great that she's here.

Mr. Grady says, "Welcome to *** who *** new to *** board. Returning members, congratulations *** *** election ***." He stands and walks to the board. His back's completely to me while he keeps talking. He writes *SPONSOR* on the board, so I copy that into my notebook. A minute later, he writes *DONATION LETTER* and underlines it four times. Obviously, a super important point. And one thing I can definitely do.

I silently start crafting a donation letter, since I still can't make out what he's saying about everything else we need to be doing. I want to ask him to please turn around, but I look at Mom—who's walking in late with another class sponsor—and realize I can't give her an additional reason to insist on the implants. So for now, I fake it, while trying to read the notes that Sabrina's writing, but no luck there either.

Even when he turns around, Mr. Grady's still so far at the other end of the room that I can barely make out any words. For once, I *almost* wish I'd slipped my SurfCon into his shirt pocket. Honestly, Mom probably would've done it herself if she'd gotten here on time.

I will myself to concentrate on his sentences. I watch his lips to see the formations as words pass through. But it's useless. Maybe if I knew for sure which sounds I don't typically hear, I'd be better at faking this.

I have to prove to Mom that I can still do this job successfully. It's not like my hearing's *that* much worse than last year.

I wonder exactly how bad it might be this time next year. Like, what specifically will I not hear then that I can hear right now? And the year after that?

These thoughts make it more real. What if I can never be on student government again? Or any other club? Just like I can't surf anymore.

When I think of losing my hearing in general, I feel like I can deal, because I have so far. But when I think in specifics, it's like my whole world is slipping away. How do you learn to live in a world not actually built for you? The thought nearly suffocates me. I excuse myself to the bathroom, though not as embarrassingly as I did after the speeches. At least if I'm not in the classroom, I'll have a legit reason to ask Mom exactly what Mr. Grady's asking us to do.

CHAPTER 9

R-Jarrow's blaring in my ears, and I can't stop thinking about her new album—or maybe just a song—dropping in five days. Yesterday, she posted six carousel horses wearing pink flower necklaces. And today's post was five girls on unicycles. I wish September thirteenth would hurry up and get here already.

I bounce on my bed. *You gotta live . . . live free* blares through my aids, and I sing the chorus at the top of my lungs. Lucky sleeps through it all.

When I flip around mid-bounce, Mom and Dad are standing in my room. I land butt-first on my bed and vault toward my phone to turn it off. "Sorry," I say. "Was I singing too loud?"

The weird look on their faces doesn't disappear, so there must be another reason they're in my room.

"What's wrong?" I ask.

Dad sits on my desk chair. Mom straightens the comforter on my bed before taking a seat near my pillows. She pats the space next to her, but I don't feel like sitting. Not when their faces say they have bad news before their mouths can.

Dad starts, "*** *** was great today. She—"

His lips keep moving, but all I hear is *beep, beep* in my right ear. My hearing aid battery is about to die.

"She *** *** *** *** questions ready—"

Beep, beep. "Hold on," I say and open my desk drawer, but I'm out of ear batteries. "I need to go to the kitchen." They follow me there. It only takes a second to change the battery, and when I put the aid back in, I try to process everything I've already missed. "Can you start over, please? And talk clearly?"

"Sorry," he says. "Let's sit."

We head to the living room, and my stomach instantly goes sour. I can clearly make out a mildew smell, and considering how much it rained at the end of summer, this probably isn't a good thing. My parents sit on the couch, and I plop into an oversized chair across from them.

Dad says, "Mom called that place in Orlando a few days ago, but it took a while for them to call back. She had a whole list of questions ready for Dr. Brandt."

I look to her. "You called?"

"Yes," she says. "I wasn't sure they'd put Dr. Brandt on *** phone directly, but I was ready in case. And I *** speak *** her. *** sounds like *** intelligent woman doing great work."

My stomach feels bubbly, like ginger ale when I open a new bottle and the fizz creeps up the inside, trying to decide if it's going to settle or explode. I'm afraid to open my mouth and ask the bazillion questions I have, in case that fizz bubbles over.

"*** so sorry." Mom shakes her head. "Dr. Brandt *is* studying cases like yours, but *** too old for her trial."

I shake my head right back. "No. She just needs to meet me. She'll see I'm worth including."

Dad stands, opening his arms, but I burrow into my chair and yell, "She does! She needs to meet me. She needs to know how important this is to me." Suddenly, that fizz is rumbling in my gut, bubbling into my throat. "She needs to hear how I'm embarrassed that I have to sit up front and hand over my SurfCon in every single class. How I can't even surf anymore." How Troy would probably like me if these things weren't stuck in my ears. How I'm probably going to have to give up student government next year. But I don't dare say those last two out loud.

Mom looks away, and Dad sits again, burying his face in his palms. They know I'm right. They know it's worth the trip.

Mom says, "I tried. I really ***. Your dad *** I were actually hopeful when *** found *** study, but you're just not *** candidate."

"But—"

"There's more." Mom pulls a pillow to her chest. "I did discuss *** situation *** Dr. Brandt. She thinks it's possible, since *** have *** loss *** Colby doesn't, *** *** it's from the *** ear infections you had over the years. Sometimes *** types of antibiotic drops *** cause cochlear hairs to die ***."

Her words take a while to make sense in my head, but when they do, I can hardly believe it. "Are you saying my hearing loss might be because of a medicine that was actually supposed to help me?"

"It's possible," she says.

"And no one told you this before you put the drops in my ears?"

Dad raises his voice. "No one's to blame *** this.

And there's no guarantee that's what caused your hearing loss. The government approved *** medication. Essentially *** drops were safe, though they may have affected *** people differently."

"So they approved a medicine that killed the hairs in some people's ears? That's so unfair! They shouldn't allow a medicine like that to be given at all. It's like gambling."

Mom gives me an upside-down smile.

"Why are you looking at me like that?"

"Think *** it," she says. "That medicine *** approved *** some people still *** terrible side effects."

"Yeah . . ." But now I get it. Stem cells. "Well, I don't care if the stem cell stuff doesn't work. And even if it makes my ears worse, you're already convinced that's going to happen anyway. We should at least try this. Before the implant."

Dad says, "What *** the side effect *** losing your eyesight or something else? We just won't know till it's been around *** many years, and right now it's not even available at all. The implants *have* been around for years. We know the minimal risks, but also the high success rate. It's a safer and more reliable option."

I shake my head, over and over.

Dad adds, "Science *** great, but it's not always foolproof. A person needs to be careful. Not be *** first to try something new."

"Okay," I say. "But technology moves fast. Just look at the new phones that come out every year. I'm sure the medical people won't approve stem cells until they're sure it works and there are no dangerous side effects. But that's not going to take ten years. Or even five."

I pause for effect, but also because the smell makes my nostrils want to vomit. This could help my case and prove to Mom and Dad that I'm smarter than they know, so I add, "And by the way, we must have a leak somewhere, because I can plain-as-day smell mold, like in Grandma's basement."

Both are silent, eyes wide. For a while, no one says anything, but Mom's giving Dad a look while Dad glances at the roof and baseboards to see if I'm right.

Eventually Mom says, "Dr. Brandt said *** there *** no definite stem cell transplant or gene therapy available right now, *** because *** losing your hearing *** fast, she agrees that—"

"No!" I scream. "Don't say it."

"I'm sorry. We *** this is hard," she says. "But Dr. Brandt agrees cochlear implants *are* the best option for ***. It's *** best way to improve *** quality of life."

"Why do you keep saying that? What does it even mean? Because once you put those things in my head, I'll never really be me again. Is that what you mean by quality?" I push out of my seat and pace in front of them. "Did you know some people get blood that collects around the implant site? Or that brain fluid could start to leak? Did you know my tinnitus could get worse? Worse than it already is! Forget eating, because lots of people with implants say food doesn't taste the same anymore."

Dad starts to say something, but I cut him off.

"And here's my favorite complication. Did you know that sometimes manufacturers go out of business? So if something breaks on that bionic implant later on, I could be stuck with this thing for the rest of my whole life and not even have anyone that can fix it because they decided to abandon their patients and move to a nice beach somewhere."

"Rayne!" Dad tries to reach for me.

"Oh," I add. "And balloons. I can never be around balloons again, because did you know that static electricity can mess with the implants too? But sure, put them in my head, because this all sounds like they'll give me a much better *quality of life*."

Mom wipes tears from her face. "Not all *** that *** true anymore. Like *** said yourself, technology moves fast, *** CIs have come *** long way. I promise. I've researched *** heck out *** ***."

"Even if some of it's true, even if only one of those things is true, why would you make me go through that?" My whole body shakes. Fear prickles my skin like hail pelting cars in a summer storm, while the tears fall just as furiously.

Dad pulls me into him, enveloping me in his arms and not letting go, even though I'm trying my hardest to break free.

When he finally lets me go, he raises my face to his and says, "We feel awful about your ears. And if either of us could have this problem instead of you, believe me, we'd take it. The fact is, we can't change it, but as your parents, we'd be foolish not to help you. And that may not be in the way *** think is best. Being a parent isn't always easy. *** fact, sometimes it downright stinks. Like *** situation, because I know you don't want *** implants, but we have to make *** right choice for you. We listened to your side about stem cells, we looked into it, but *** best option for you to have the best life possible is still *** implants."

I pull away and hope my words will sound as smart as possible. "You shouldn't get to make that choice for me. I'm not a baby. I know what I have to gain and lose with each of the options. You think I'm not old enough to understand everything, but I am. And they're my ears. It should only be up to me."

He clears his throat. "Look. We're *** open to exploring options—"

"See what I mean?" I cut him off. "Your mind's already made up."

"What?" He shakes his head. "I just said we *are still* open."

"You did?" I may have missed a word in there. "Thank you." I sit again.

"Sorry." He clears his throat. "We're still open to other options, but your appointment with Dr. Olsen at Dade University is a week from tomorrow. He's the best of the best. Trust me."

One week? No. Just no! "I'm not going," I say. Why can't Colby be here when I need him? He'd agree with me.

"Honey." Mom kneels in front of me, but I

sink deeper into my chair. "We just want *** to meet him."

Puzzle pieces start clicking in my head. "But you only talked to Dr. Brandt *today*. How do you already have an appointment with Dr. Olsen?"

Mom says, "We've had *** appointment for *** few months."

"Months?" I yell.

She clarifies, "Since *** beginning *** summer."

"Seriously?" I yell again. I don't even think my hearing was that bad back then.

Dad says, "For now, we just want you to talk to him. Then we'll discuss it again."

"And what if I still don't want the surgery after I've talked to him?" I ask.

Mom looks at my feet and inches back to her spot on the couch next to Dad. She says, "With *** latest tests, the insurance approved *** very quickly. Quicker *** we imagined. *** wanted *** to do *** surgery *** soon *** possible, but we put it *** *** December, to give *** time to meet Dr. Olsen *** *** *** people *** implants. We *** thinking *** ***. We can always cancel, but . . ."

They've already scheduled the surgery? Without even telling me? December's only three months away. "No! No, no, no, no, no!" The inside of my head is full of static. Panic's swirling so fast it's making me dizzy. I can't be here. With them. In this house. It sucks that the one place where I should feel the safest and the okay-est is at home. But I don't. I haven't in a long time. And I'm beginning to wonder if I ever will again.

I bolt for the door.

CHAPTER 10

Outside, I catch my breath. I force myself to stay calm. I have to. Because I'm going to fight them on this. And I'm going to win.

The moon is hardly even a sliver. The closest streetlight is six houses away, which helps hide me—squished against the beige, stucco front wall of our house. I don't want to make it easy for Mom and Dad to find me when they come looking.

But they don't come. I lie on the grass, face up, searching for my Delphinus—it'll only be visible for a few more weeks since it's a seasonal constellation. I want to make a wish, but it's been a long time since one of mine's come true. Instead, I make a *hope* on my five shiny stars. *I hope no one else ever loses their hearing over some dumb medicine and that someday I'll feel like me again.*

I close my eyes and take deep breaths until my

insides calm down. I want to text Jenika. She'd know what to do. But the light on my phone will give me away if Mom happens to be looking out the window.

Suddenly it hits me why Mom didn't come looking. She's probably tracking my phone. She must know I'm just outside the door.

Frustration bubbles in my stomach again. I'm so tired of being a kid. I should turn off the GPS and just go to Jenika's. That'll show them how independent I really am. But it's already so dark. Who knows what's between her house and me?

"What *** *** ***?"

I jump higher than a grasshopper.

I'm ready to sprint to the front door when I hear, "It's ***, Troy."

I squint. His tall body's shadowed by the faint streetlight that's a ways behind him. Now that my heartbeat's slowing again, I recognize his wide shoulders and his voice.

"What are you doing scaring me like that?" I ask.

"I called *** name, but I could tell *** didn't hear me." He's overly enunciating every word. "So I was just coming closer to talk to you. I tried to make *** noise to give *** a warning." He jams his hands into his pockets.

These broken ears. I fluff the hair on the sides of my head, hoping to cover my aids. I definitely wasn't lucky enough to get thick hair. A few pieces of grass fall. "Sorry. I guess . . . well, never mind. What are you doing out so late anyway?"

"Swim practice ran late, *** then I had homework, but I needed to talk to ***. You keep avoiding me *** school and *** don't answer my texts." He rocks onto his tiptoes and then onto his heels.

It's true, I've avoided his texts, but only because he and Lourdes are always together now. Even if we're friends and he cares about my ears, I don't want him around until I can get the minnows in my stomach to go away whenever I think about him. "Oh," I say. "How was practice?"

"Good." He points to the grass. "Want to sit?"

"I guess." I mean, I'm not in the best mood, but if he came all this way, I should do the right thing and listen. But no talking, since lately, my words never make sense when he's around.

After he sits, I move to his right, the streetlight behind me lighting his face, so I can read his lips. We both cross our legs, crisscross applesauce, and it's like we're back in kindergarten during circle time, only with a lot more awkwardness.

He rolls a blade of grass between his palms. "I've got insider information." He's careful to pronounce each word, and I appreciate his effort to be clear but not slow. The people who talk slowly to me make me feel even dumber.

I'm hoping my super-ears haven't misunderstood him. Jenika and her mom always say that the gossip at their hair salon is juicier than the raw meat at a butcher shop. For once, I may actually get to know something before them. I plan my words. "About what?"

"*** heard Mr. Grady tell someone today that *** won by *** landslide."

If he's right, I'm surprised.

He goes on, "I know *** don't like to talk about your hearing, but it's no big deal that *** didn't hear Quinton's question. I could barely hear ***. Still, I felt bad when people laughed, *** I tried to find you after, but you'd disappeared. People know you're *** best for the job. I wanted *** be sure *you* know that."

If they knew I couldn't hear a darn thing in the Harvest Fest meeting, they'd definitely regret voting for me.

He says, "After you left, I also had to use *** bathroom, so I crossed my jiggling legs, announced my need to the whole room, and then excused myself while I hopped out the door. It's actually quite *** proper thing to do, don't *** think? Otherwise, people could assume *** person's rude for simply up and leaving, when really they just had to pee."

At first, I think he's joking. Jenika would have told me about this—unless she didn't want to remind me of my own abrupt exit. In my head, I picture the scene Troy must've made, and I can't help it: I crack up. I fall back on the grass and laugh till I'm practically crying. When I open my eyes, Troy's lying next to me.

"Sorry," I say. "But that was hilarious."

We're both facing skyward.

"No big deal. I've been laughed at before."

"So you say. Maybe your gaming business will actually be a hit."

Out of the blue, he says, "Seriously, though, people don't just like ***, Rayne. They love you. You're legit nice *** everyone." He looks at me, reaches for my hand, and goes back to staring at the sky.

It's a good thing the moon decided to play hooky tonight, 'cause I'm sure my cheeks are pink. I notice how well our hands go together. How they fit just right.

"*** *** *kay?"

My heart skips as I try to figure out what he asked. "Yes, this is great."

"Sorry." He turns his head to face me. "I asked if you're okay. You don't have to talk about it if you don't want to, but it's okay if you do."

I close my eyes, feeling dumb all over again. But he squeezes my fingers, and I realize it's not like he left when I had my sobfest on the beach. Maybe he doesn't mind that I can't hear well. "Yeah," I whisper, forcing the words past the lump in my throat. "I am okay." More than okay, at least for now. I'm definitely letting go of the brakes tonight.

He raises our linked hands and points with one of his fingers. "See that orange-looking star?"

It's easy to follow the direction he's pointing, with my own hand intertwined with his. "Yeah. It's called Arcturus."

"Wait!" He sits up and lets go of my hand. "*** know about it?"

"Well, it's part of the Boötes constellation, so yeah." Troy's hated science for as long as he's been alive, so I'm surprised by this sudden interest in astronomy.

"Okay, Star Girl." He shakes his head fast. "But do *** *know*, know about it? Like, the story behind it?"

I don't know that one, actually. I shake my head.

"***, I've been studying the stars."

"Really? What for?"

He looks at me funny. "I don't know." He lies down next to me and grabs my hand again. "So I *** sound smart *** I'm telling *** about them."

A thousand minnows swish through my stomach, and I feel light, like I might actually lift off the earth and float right up to that star.

"So do *** want to know the story *** it *** not?"

I smile. "Yeah."

"Good!" He rolls onto his side so he's facing me, speaking clearly, but never letting go of my hand. If my heart could smile, it would. He goes on, "Once upon a time, there was this coyote, and he was trying to impress some girls. So he took out his eyeballs and juggled them. The girls went wild, and they cheered so loud he accidentally tossed one eyeball way into the sky, and it got stuck there." He points toward the star again and says, "That's his eyeball right there."

I laugh, careful not to laugh *at* him. I mean, I know star lore is bizarre, but still, I wonder if he made this up.

"What *** way to pick up chicks, right?" he asks.

"I guess if you're a coyote." I snort. "So, what else do you know? Tell me about another star."

"Oh, sorry. That's *** I've got." He flips over. "Maybe it's not *** cool as your dolphin but—"

"No." I stop him. "It's definitely just as cool." I picture the eyeball star again, and when I laugh this time, a genuine happiness fills my whole body. I'm really, really glad Troy came over.

Forget about the ridiculous romance stuff the girls in my class used to talk about at slumber parties—before I stopped going, because once those lights are shut off and they keep talking, I can't follow anything they're saying. Most of the girls claimed that the perfect date involves makeup, heels, a fancy dinner, and dancing. Only two disagreed. I didn't know what to think at the time, but now I know I'd rather lie here on the grass and hear about a coyote who flung his eyeball clear into the solar system than dress up and go to some fancy dinner any day.

And I'd swear Arcturus is winking at Troy and me.

———

I remember when I first learned to surf. Colby had to put me on the board in the shallow and drag me out past the break. I was scared of being attacked by an octopus. Not a shark—I knew they wouldn't eat me since I'm warm-blooded—but an octopus. Okay, so maybe they wouldn't eat me either, but they had eight tentacles that could easily wrap around my body and suffocate me. So yeah, I wanted to surf, mostly to hang with Colby and just be in the water, but the idea of an octopus getting me gave me the heebie-jeebies, even if it didn't actually make logical sense.

It felt great to be out there. To catch waves and thrills all at once. But the minute I fell off, terror jolted my whole body, and I'd scramble till I was either back on my board or on land. Still, I kept surfing because I hoped that eventually the fear would go away. The excitement of riding was too great to stop. And I decided to learn more about octopuses in hopes it would help me be less afraid. It worked.

I feel like that girl just learning to surf again now. Hanging out with Troy, winning the election, and having Jenika as a best friend are all like catching the epic wave, but underneath that board, underneath the water I can't see through, it feels like a threat is waiting for me. And as much as I want to focus on Troy, my brain won't let me enjoy that ride.

I text Colby on the way to school. I wish he were here to help me balance in this new murky water.

Me: *Can you talk? Mom and Dad are being ridiculous.*

Colby: *Can I call you this weekend? Studying for a test now.*

Me: *Sure. Good luck.*

I've decided to avoid all my friends at school today. I just can't deal right now. And the best way to make sure I'm left alone is to fake a major migraine.

Jenika knows my aids sometimes give me bad headaches, so I know she won't force any conversations today. Troy says he understands when I dramatically rub my temples in homeroom, but I'm not sure he really believes me. Maybe he'll think I just didn't like talking with him last night. Maybe it's easier to let him think that. My life's way too complicated right now anyway. But I can still kinda feel his hand in mine. And I already miss it.

By the end of the day, I'm more than ready to go home and lock myself in my room with Lucky. I'll watch movies. Figure out the R-Jarrow clues. And enjoy not talking to anyone. For the whole weekend.

On my way out of school, I see Jenika duck into the bathroom. She looks upset. I wonder what happened. She's tough, though. Whatever it is, I'm sure she'll be fine.

I push through the door to head outside, but suddenly my feet won't move. I can't leave. I can't do that to her.

In the bathroom, her back's pressed against the tile wall, eyes closed, and I can tell she's doing some sort of deep breathing.

"Are you okay?" I ask.

She jumps. "Ray! *** scared me. *** look pale. *** sure you're not getting sick? Wait . . ." She pulls her volleyball uniform shirt over her mouth and nose like the total germaphobe she is. "*** *** *** *** ***."

"I'm not sick." I tug her shirt down. "I lied about my headache. And you're the one who looks bad right now."

"You lied?" She backs away anyway.

"I just wanted some space."

"You had to avoid *me*? Your best friend."

"Trust me, it's not about you." I want to tell her what's been going on. I should have from the beginning, but it was easier not to. And now, I can see she's got her own stuff going on. "I'll fill you in later. What's wrong?"

"I think Coach A wants me *** quit. I think he's being *** horrible human to get me to leave *** purpose."

"Why would he do that? You're the best one out there."

"I think he thinks *** girls like me as *** coach better than him. It's not my fault they ask me *** serving and hitting tips. I don't randomly offer advice. They ask. I want to win, so I show them."

"Everyone knows you've played club forever and how good you are. Of course they're asking you. He's just jealous. He's new, so maybe he thinks you make him look bad."

"He's an adult. He's not jealous *** me." She stuffs her clothes in her bag.

"Sure sounds like it." I'm glad this is all it is. I know she'll be fine soon, and I can go home to my room and hibernate.

"Well, whatever he ***, I'm done. I'm tired *** him singling me out and yelling at me and picking on me during practice. Yesterday's game was *** worst. And today, he already *** I'm running extra for missing a dig. All day I thought I'd push through, but every minute closer to practice time, my brain just gets hotter *** hotter. I swear I'm quitting." She's practically hyperventilating.

I've never seen her so fired up, and I feel horrible for not being there for her all day. I grab her shoulders. "Take another breath." She does, and I say, "You love volleyball. You are the best one out there. He knows it, even if he won't admit it. And the team needs you. You can't just leave them hanging."

"I don't know, Ray. *** he says one thing today, I'll lose it. I'll probably say something awful *** get suspended. I just can't."

I want my bed. My room. My dog. I want to hide in total quiet. But it will have to wait. "You can because I'm coming with you."

"What?"

"I'm going to practice. Whenever you're about to lose it with him, come over and let me have it. Say anything you want to me. Then get out on the court and play."

"Seriously?"

I cross my arms over my chest. "Do I look like I'm joking?"

She hugs me. "You really are *** best."

On the way to volleyball, I see Mr. Faro, and I tell Jenika I'll meet her in the gym.

I pause in front of the open door of the storage room and wave.

Mr. Faro waves back.

With my hand flat, I touch my fingertips—palm side in—to my chin, then move my hand forward and down. I add a smile, so he knows I mean it.

He replies with a thumbs up and says, "You're welcome. You know, I could stand to learn *** sign for that."

"I'll be sure to look it up. Meanwhile . . ." I touch my thumb to the rest of my fingers and lift my arm above my head. I make a small circle in the air and then open my fingers as I drop my hand downward just a little bit toward Mr. Faro.

His eyes are wide, like he's trying to figure it out.

It's bothered me so much ever since he said he felt like a shadow. "You are sunlight. At least to me."

Before I turn to leave, he signs *Thank you*, and I'd swear his eyes looked just the tiniest bit watery.

CHAPTER 11

I didn't want to sleep over, but Jenika insisted we celebrate her making it through the whole practice without getting in trouble. Mom wasn't thrilled, but Dad convinced her I could use some time away. Besides, she keeps saying I'm cutting all my friends off, and this is me being my regular old self. I'll try my best to celebrate, but honestly, I'm still reeling about the surgery.

I strap on Lucky's leash, and we run all the way to the Jacksons' house—she loves sleeping there too. We're both panting when I knock.

Mrs. Jackson opens the big red front door, and their dog, Putter, charges out, barking up a storm while my silent pup sniffs Putter's butt. Putter sniffs back, and soon the two are rolling around on the grass. Watching them makes me laugh and reminds me of lying on the grass with Troy last night. Of course, we weren't sniffing each other or anything gross like that.

Mrs. Jackson must notice me grinning because she says, "Well, aren't you in a great mood."

Instantly, my smile falls, almost like I shouldn't be happy with all that's going on.

She says, "I've seen wind change *** fast as your face." She leads me inside. "Something *** want to chat about?"

To be honest, I've always been a little jealous of Jenika because her mom is easy to talk to. She's a great listener, instead of always controlling the conversation. "Isn't it weird how you can feel two completely different ways at the same time?" I ask.

"Honey, don't let those mixed-up feelings put *** knot in your rope. That's simply called life." She's careful to enunciate her words for me, so I can understand despite her thick southern drawl, as she calls it. It makes me happy that she remembers to do that for me, without making a big deal of it.

We pass through the living room, which is decked out in nautical stuff and reminds me of some of the yachts we toured once when Jenika's dad took us to a boat show for his work. I like that this house is bright—it makes it easier for me to see people's faces. The dogs follow us to the kitchen, licking each other's faces as they go.

Mrs. Jackson points to a barstool. "Sit. How about *** chocolate chip cookies to fill the part *** you that isn't so happy this afternoon?"

Unless they're magic cookies—which they might be, knowing her baking—I doubt they'll make me feel better. But I am hungry. "That sounds delicious. Thank you."

Jenika flops onto a stool next to me, her braids piled in a messy bun on top of her head. "Thanks for coming to practice."

"Always." Although I'm really glad to finally be away from the gym's echoing voices and shrieky whistle. They made my head want to explode.

Mrs. Jackson asks, "Have *** girls decided who you're doing *** biography project on?"

Jenika swallows a cookie. "I'm doing Ruth Bader Ginsburg. That girl was not afraid to speak her mind."

I'm not surprised by her choice at all, though I hadn't asked her about it myself.

She takes a sip of milk and adds, "I'm trying *** get Rayne to *** Helen Keller." I roll my eyes and she play-punches me as she says, "No lie, Rayne, she *** a boss! She ate up anyone who dissed her."

Okay, so I didn't know that. And sure, it sounds intriguing, her confidence and all. If it's true. But still, I say, "Thanks. I have other options to consider."

"Suit ***self." She waves me off.

Mrs. Jackson says, "She's fascinating! But I can understand why she might not be *** cup *** tea, Rayne. I'm pretty sure she *** said she'd rather be blind than deaf."

"Well, that's . . . wait . . ." I say the words again in my head. "For real?" If I had to pick one of the two—like pick one or *die*—I'm pretty sure I'd choose deaf over blind. "That's weird, but maybe it's because Helen lived in old-fashioned times. At least I can still communicate without hearing too well, thanks to email, captions, texting, even fancy glasses at the movie theater."

Mrs. Jackson nods. "If I remember right, she said that *** problems of deafness felt more complex to her than *** problems of blindness. I don't know *** everyone would agree *** that, though she certainly had *** informed opinion!"

"Exactly," Jenika says. "And *** don't have to agree with her to think she's interesting. *** girl had depth, Ray. I still have *** book you gave back *** *** want to borrow it again."

Mrs. Jenkins smiles at me, and I try to look happy, but I don't want to think about the report right now. The weight of the surgery keeps getting heavier by the minute.

Jenika nods toward her room, so her mom doesn't see. She can probably tell I need to talk with her in private.

I nod back, and we scarf down the cookies as fast as possible.

———

The evening sun's bursting through the four windows in Jenika's room, making her lime-green walls practically glow. The black furniture looks awesome against the green. I never would've picked those two colors to go together, but Jenika's good like that. The dogs, who followed us, cuddle next to each other in the sun-spot that's warming a shaggy purple rug on the floor.

"*** what's going on?" She plunks herself down on an oversized zebra-print chair.

I sit on her bed and tell her about Mom calling Dr. Brandt and her not letting me in the study. And how Mom and Dad started secretly planning for my surgery months ago. Months! Jenika's gasping with my every word—not to be theatrical or anything, though it sometimes looks that way. It's just how she reacts when something burns her up.

I add, "I was so mad, I ran right out of the house. I only made it to my front yard, though. Why am I such a chicken?" I shake my head. "Anyway, guess what?"

"Don't *** dare make me guess. This is *** too intense."

"Fine. Troy came to see me."

Her eyes do that bug-out thing again. "Yeah?"

"He said he wanted me to know nearly everyone voted for me. Then he held my hand while we talked about the stars."

"Stars! Ha!" Jenika's clapping and twirling in circles, maybe happier about this than I am. I mean, I'm happy for now, but there's a strong possibility that once my parents force me to get the implants, Troy won't like me anymore—at least not like *that*.

"I knew it!" she squeals. Putter barks and hops around Jenika's feet. Lucky doesn't move at all. Lazy dog. "But wait, you kept this from me all day?"

"I haven't even been able to focus on it much myself. All I can really think about is that in three months my parents are going to ruin my life."

"Come ***. You're not giving up, *** you? That's not like you."

"What am I supposed to do? I'm trying my best to fight them, but I'm running out of options."

"Can't *** talk to your audiologist *** something? You said he agreed *** you about not needing implants right ***."

"I tried to ask him last time I was there. Dr. James asked to speak to me alone in the office, but Mom said no. I was so mad. I mean, it's my life. My ears. Right?"

She sits again. "I think *** should get in touch *** him."

"It's not like I can pick up the phone and call. But wait . . ." I flip to my stomach. "I could maybe ride my bike to his office." I pull out my laptop and look up Dr. James's office. "He's open tomorrow till noon."

"On *** Saturday?"

"It says so."

"I'll come *** you."

"No, I need you to stay here and keep my phone. My mom can track me."

"Right. I'll pretend *** you if she texts."

"Perfect." Actually, it's more than perfect, because there's something else I've been wanting to ask him about too.

"And meanwhile *** should be able to look up if *** parents can make *** get surgery." She scooches me over on the bed, and her fingers fly across the keyboard: *Can parents force a kid to have a medical operation?* There's no exact match, but she clicks on a link that says, *Does my child have a right to refuse medical treatment?* Close enough.

Jenika points, and I click the link for *Gillick competence*. She reads out loud over my shoulder, while I follow along. "Whether or not a child is capable of giving the necessary consent will depend on the child's maturity and understanding and the nature of the consent required. The child must be capable of making a reasonable assessment of the advantages and disadvantages of the treatment proposed, so the consent, if given, can be properly and fairly described as true consent."

Ohmygosh. This sounds exactly like what I need. "So, all I have to do is prove I'm competent!"

"Sounds like you'll need *** lawyer," Jenika says.

"Yeah, but I bet any lawyer could see that I've got a strong case. I can show them all my report cards. You know my mom's saved every single one since kindergarten." Colby's too, along with every piece of artwork we've made since birth. Heck, she's even saved every movie stub, every airline ticket, and all those old AAA TripTik maps from every vacation we ever took. She swears they've got sentimental value.

Jenika strokes Lucky's belly. "You've always hated that *** mom saved those report cards, but I bet you're glad ***."

"I never *hated* her saving them. I like that she was proud. I was just embarrassed how she plastered them on the fridge and bragged about how smart I was to every person who stepped foot in our house." Even though I would ask her to stop. Mom would shush me and say *she* never got straight As, which makes me sometimes wonder if she showed off the report cards for the attention it gave *her*. A proud teacher with a perfect daughter. To be honest, I think that's why Mom's pushing these implants so hard. I'm definitely not getting straight As anymore, and she didn't even hang my final report card last year. I'm hardly perfect now.

I turn to a clean page in the middle of my notebook, right after the NIDCD information. I write, *Gillick competence.* "Wait." I point to the web address, which ends in *co.uk.* "I don't think this competent thing is for the US. The website's in England."

"I'm sure *** have something like it here too." Jenika leans over my laptop again and types *lawyer, Florida, Coral Springs.* She clicks the first link, for

Pembrant and Trice, PA, and we stare at the mean-looking faces of two guys dressed in suits with colored napkins sticking out of their chest pockets.

"Sorry, but no," she says.

"My thoughts exactly. Hang on . . ." I type in the search bar: *What kind of lawyer can a kid get? Coral Springs.*

I open the site for Stern, Stern, and Stern, Attorneys at Law. Even the name sounds ferocious. It'll take someone strong to battle Mom, for sure.

Mr. Stern looks like he could be my principal's twin. Neither smile. Maybe they like scaring people. He's a definite no.

The first lady-Stern who's listed has a nice face. She looks like she could be a kindergarten teacher and would give great hugs.

"I pick her," I say.

Jenika runs her finger along my computer screen, reading Ms. Stern's biography. "I *** know. It says she mainly represents women going *** divorces. But look at the other lady."

Ms. Stern No. 2, whose dark hair is pulled into a tight ponytail and who's surrounded by a boring gray background, is smiling, but only a little. She doesn't seem teacher-y at all. She's all business.

Jenika points. "What about ***?"

"I don't know. The first lady seems like she'd be nicer." I study both of their faces again. "This second one looks too young to be a mom—but maybe that's a good thing."

"Definitely good. She looks fierce."

"Oh." I point to her biography on the screen. "It says she specializes in family law." She sounds perfect. I hope she'll understand my situation and want to help. I click on the contact form and fill the whole thing out. "Look. It promises that someone will get back to me in forty-eight hours or less."

This has to be a sign that I'm doing the right thing, because I'm not good at waiting.

"Hold on!" I hop off Jenika's bed and grab a dictionary from her fancy, antique bookshelf. "We should use this to make sure I sound extra competent in the email—in case Ms. Stern has any doubt when she sees I'm only twelve."

"Good idea," she says.

When I'm finished, Jenika rereads my email draft out loud, twice. She's about to hit send when my hand slaps hers away from the computer—my breath catching in my chest so sharply I cough.

"Good Lord, what's *** matter? she asks.

"I don't know . . . just wait." I take a few belly-filling breaths. If I hit send, like actually hit the big red blinking button, I can't take it back. What if my mom and dad find out?

I mean, right now I just want to see what Ms. Stern has to say. But really, how many kids actually ask a lawyer to help them fight their parents? I picture the disappointment on my parents' faces, worse than their disappointment when the doctor first told them I had a progressive sensorineural hearing loss, and it wasn't going to get better. Mom cried that whole night, and Dad hugged her for hours telling her it would all be okay, while I watched everything go down like a movie. A bad one. One I didn't particularly feel like being part of, though I had the starring role.

I don't want to keep being a disappointment to them, or to keep making Mom upset. But worse, way worse, would be getting those awful implants. I cannot, will not get them, especially if the stem cell research might get the a-okay soon from who-ever needs to approve it. Maybe then I'd feel like me again.

I have to do this.

Have to.

"Okay. I don't have a choice."

"Yes, you do," says Jenika. "But it's just a question *** now anyway. *** should at least know *** options."

"Right. My options." I nod rapidly. "Do it. Before I change my mind. Wait, no. Let me."

Click!

I shake out my wrists. I stand and shake them some more as my heart sprints.

"You don't look *** good," Jenika says.

"I don't feel so good." I pace in front of her bed, and Lucky whimpers. I bend down and snuggle my face in hers. A few minutes later, my email pings, and my nervousness swells again when I see a reply from Stern and Stern. I suck in a deep breath, knowing my answer is one click away.

CHAPTER 12

Of course, it would be impossible for someone to type out a whole answer that fast. Instead, I've gotten a form email saying someone would respond soon. But the waiting . . . that's worse than suffering through the Box of Shame. Or close to it.

———

I'm feeling a little more hopeful, and we still need to celebrate Jenika surviving practice, so we ask her parents to take us mini-golfing. They're supposed to celebrate their anniversary tonight with dinner at home, but they agree to go to a restaurant near the mini-golf place instead. They're the best!

As much as I hate too many people being around at once, tonight's about Jenika, so I secretly text

Beth and Isabelle—one of Jenika's friends from volleyball—to come too.

They rush us when we get out of the Jacksons' car. Jenika hugs them. "What *** *** doing here?"

Beth says, "Rayne wanted *** surprise you."

Isabelle adds, "It's definitely worth celebrating that *** haven't gotten kicked *** *** team yet."

"That's for sure." Jenika loops her arms in mine and Isabelle's. I grab Beth's hand as Jenika pulls us toward the entrance. "*** make *** *** epic night."

And we do. To my relief, Beth's party doesn't come up, so there's no awkwardness about that; I know the others would be disappointed to find out I'm going to ditch it. All three of them try especially hard to make sure I can hear, and I love them so much for it. The few times I can't catch what they're saying, I spend time looking up signs for weird things on the ChannelThis phone app.

Jenika points to my phone when she hears me laughing. "What *** *** doing?"

I tell them how Mr. Faro taught me a few signs, and I decided to learn more. ChannelThis has videos of everything imaginable, so I figured they'd have sign language too. It's especially fun looking up dorky words.

"Hang on. I know what to look up." The sign is hysterical. I try to compose myself. "Ready?" I make a fist but leave my thumb sticking out. Then I tap the pinky side of my fist—that's opposite my stuck-out thumb—to the side of my forehead twice.

"What's that?" Jenika asks.

I get all serious. "It's a most perfect sign for Coach A."

Isabelle looks at my phone. "Yes, *** perfect." She laughs. "It *** jerk."

All three of us crack up right there at hole eleven, calling Coach A exactly what he is, and laughing harder than I've laughed in a really long time.

I say, "Instead of yelling at him, you can just do this whenever you get mad."

Isabelle grabs her stomach. "I *** totally see *** doing it *** *** court."

I'm pretty sure we can all picture it, which keeps us laughing, and when we finally calm down and move on to the next hole, Jenika nudges me. "See, this is just one more reason we should both learn to sign."

Back at Jenika's, I refresh my email at least ten times, but nothing pops up.

Jenika turns on R-Jarrow and yells, "I'm *** *** shower. Be back *** *** ***."

I snuggle with Lucky and Putter on her bed, but after a second I get up to turn the music louder, hoping it'll drown out the spinning thoughts crammed in my head. Tonight was great. But there's still so much else going on too.

At the amusement park, my favorite ride is the Free Fall. I love how it yanks me up like a puppet on a string, drops me a little, pulls me up again, and dangles for the slightest second before plunging me toward the ground while my stomach hangs out in my throat. Love it. Like so much.

Usually.

The last twenty-four hours have felt the same way, all up-in-the-air-happy when Troy held my hand, then plunging—not in a fun, rollercoaster way—when I think of the surgery. And today, all happy to find a lawyer and hang out at mini-golf, but now out of my mind waiting for a reply and thinking of how to talk to Dr. James tomorrow. How can one whole day be both perfect and perfectly terrible? I just wish the ride would end, because the falling part doesn't feel good at all.

There's still no email on Saturday morning, and I'm seriously losing my mind. I'm running out of time before my meeting with Dr. Olsen next week. As much as I hate the idea of hurting Mom and Dad, if Ms. Stern says she can help, I already know I'll work with her. Mom might not take it seriously, but I hope Dad will, and that he'll get Mom to change her mind. He has to. Because I'm not changing mine.

Jenika says, "I'll cover *** you while you meet Dr. James, but then we need to get *** mind off this, since I doubt lawyers work *** weekends. We should keep busy today."

"And tomorrow too." I didn't mean to say that out loud.

"Did *** forget? Tomorrow's Beth's party."

"Right. Yeah."

Jenika grabs clothes and goes into her bathroom. She's so lucky to have one right in her room. I hear her mumbling, "*** *** *** *** *** *** *** ***."

Part of me wants to yell at her, but instead I just ignore her.

"Sorry, sorry!" She comes out in a bikini. "I asked

what you're wearing to Beth's party. Check out this
*** bathing suit my mom bought ***."

Jenika looks fantastic in the aqua bikini. "You're
on fire," I say.

She bobbles her head and struts around the room.
"Thanks. I *** love it." She checks herself out in the
mirror on the wall. "What about you? Want to borrow *** suit? Although I do love your purple one."

"I can't go. Family stuff." I move from the bed
and sit next to Putter and Lucky.

"*** *** such a liar. Come on, Ray. It'll be fine. I
won't leave *** side *** whole time. I promise."

"Who says I'm lying?"

"I do. You're not even speaking to *** parents
right now. And you just said *** *** need something
to keep *** busy *** Sunday. I've got a brain, you
know?"

I avoid looking at her.

"You *** fine last night. I'm coming to get *** at
noon. *** better be ready, or I'm going to tie *** up
and drag *** *** me."

Before this hearing junk started, I'd have laughed
at this. Jenika's stubborn. And even though last night
was a blast, and I mostly heard everything, it wasn't a
pool party. I know Jenika would keep me company,

but she shouldn't have to be stuck babysitting me. Plus, I'm sure the whole volleyball team will be there. Jenika should hang with them.

"Tomorrow!" She wags her finger near my face and walks back to the bathroom.

Just as I'm about to leave, my phone dings.

Troy: *Hope you're feeling better. Did you see Arcturus last night?*

Me: *Forgot to look.* :/

I don't know why I say this. I did see it at mini-golf. But I can't deal with Troy right now on top of everything else.

Troy: *Careful. Arcturus will fling his eyeball down at you if you make him mad.*

I laugh.

Jenika comes back out. "What's so funny?"

"It's Troy. He's talking about the eyeball star."

"I really love the idea *** you two."

"Stop," I say. "I've got way too much going on to worry about a boy."

"You're just afraid, that's ***. But Troy, he's solid. Come ***, you know this."

Me: *How's the gaming? Famous yet?*

Troy: *These things take time! Getting cameras today. See you at Beth's tomorrow?*

I pace. I don't want to lie. But as great as the other night was with him, a tiny part of my stomach is sick because he doesn't know how bad my ears actually are, and how bad they're going to get. If I'll never be my old self again, we can't be our usual us, and why would he want someone like that?

I delete the conversation without answering, so that Jenika won't happen to see it while I'm gone. "Here, I'm leaving. Promise to only answer if it's my mom!"

Jenika grabs my phone. "Promise." She holds up her crossed fingers.

I smack her hand. "Sometimes you make me so mad!"

"Yeah, but then you get over it." She blows me a kiss as I walk out the door.

CHAPTER 13

I'm not exactly nervous as I pedal toward Dr. James's office, but I keep thinking about the lawyer, and I wish I could talk to Colby about it—though if he disagrees with what I'm doing, he'll tell Mom and Dad. Then my chance will be over before it even starts.

When I get to the office, the receptionist isn't there, but Dr. James sees me through his glass window and comes out. "Is everything okay, Rayne? Where are your parents?"

"I was hoping to talk to you privately if that's okay."

"Do they know you're here?"

I shake my head.

"It wouldn't be right to talk without permission from one of your parents."

"Please," I beg. "I really need to talk to someone who understands."

He crosses his arms over his chest. "I don't know. I mean, you *are* my patient." He thinks for a minute. "I want you to know, I'm not going to offer any advice. I'm very clear on your mother's feelings. But you can ask me questions."

"Deal," I say.

We sit in the waiting room. "There's no one else here today. Saturdays are pretty slow, but I stay open for those who can't make it during the week."

"That's nice of you."

"What brings you here?"

I start with the easier part—a question that's been in the back of my mind for months. "Sometimes I think there's something wrong with me. I mean, something more than just not being able to hear. Like my brain is messed up because of my ears. Does that happen? Does hearing loss make a person's brain go bad?"

"Hearing loss does have certain effects on the brain. But explain what you mean, so I can clarify for you."

I lean forward, trying to find the words to describe this. "I can't actually tell what I can still hear versus what I just guess on—even though I can figure out sentences. I think something's wrong with my brain. I mean, I should know what I hear and what I don't hear, right?" I'm hoping his answer will help me guess a little better in conversations, so everyone will just stop worrying about me.

He smiles. "I'm happy to report that your brain is fine. This is actually a phenomenon that we call auditory closure. You're using visual and context clues when auditory alone isn't enough. These are combined with the inflection of a person's voice— things like pitch, pattern, and rhythm—which you use without even realizing it to fill in the gaps. Essentially, your brain registers all of this as hearing, even if you just deduced it based on the clues."

"So my brain figures out the words it misses and then assumes it heard those words?"

He crosses his arms over his chest. "Exactly. The brain is a wondrous organ. Even people with near-perfect hearing rely on auditory closure, but you even more so. It can be exhausting."

I sigh. "You can say that again." I've been feeling pretty dumb about this. It's a relief knowing that it's just part of the hearing loss. That there's not something else wrong with me too.

"The other thing I want to know is . . ."

"Yes?" he says when I pause. I can tell my first

question has gotten him warmed up. He's feeling more comfortable about talking to me without my parents around. Which is good, because I need him to be honest with me about this next part, especially in case I don't hear from Ms. Stern.

I take a deep breath. "Can my parents make me have the implant surgery if I don't want it?"

His eyes crease in the corner as he pulls his mouth into a tight line. Finally, he says, "I really hope it won't come to that. And to be honest, I can't answer that for certain. But—"

I cut him off, desperate to plead my case. "My parents know I don't want implants. They know I want to wait for stem cell research. They think I'm a baby and don't seem to care about me at all."

I twist my fingers together and look at the fish tank behind the counter, so I don't have to look at him. The lie's left a lump in my throat. I swallow it away. "Okay, that's not totally true. They do care. But they think their way is the right way. That the cochlear implants are the *best* answer."

"Your parents have valid reasons for insisting on the implants."

No, no, no. Please don't agree with them. Almost two weeks ago he said the opposite.

He must see the panic on my face because he quickly adds, "I've given them a lot of literature. I've answered questions for the last two years. They are definitely educating themselves. I've even slipped in additional resource options for them to consider whenever I could."

My nose burns, but I shake that away and focus. "What kind of resource options?"

"Sign language classes and updated genetic testing. Things like that."

"What's genetic testing for?"

"There are about fifty to a hundred genes involved in a functioning ear. Sometimes a mutation *** one or more genes causes hearing loss. It's good to know what's missing to help you find *** best way to proceed, especially down the road for stem cells. But even if you do the testing, there's still no current cure *** your loss. Implants don't cure deafness, but they can help you hear."

"But that's not definite. It doesn't even work for some people."

He nods. "It's a small percentage, but yes."

"I don't want to be in that percent. I don't want to take a chance when I can still hear right now. Why would anyone risk that?"

He closes his eyes and turns away, shaking his head. After a deep breath, he faces me again. "Look, your mom called me after you discovered Dr. Brandt's study and they turned you down. She asked if I knew of any other similar studies that you might qualify for. I told her how to search for some, and I've asked around too, but so far, nothing."

It should make me feel better that Mom's trying, but it doesn't. "All she has to do is cancel the operation, and then we can figure the rest out. Together. Not her and my dad deciding things without me. Don't you agree?"

I swear he nods before he catches himself and instead runs a hand through his hair. "Here's what I will say. As you know, your parents want the implants partially because they see you pulling away from friends and social situations. Things that you used to love."

"But they're wrong."

"Maybe so, but it's worthwhile to pay attention to the decisions you make." He pauses. "No matter what happens, you shouldn't hide. Don't lock yourself away."

"I promise I'm not. I just won president of my class."

"Congratulations. That's wonderful."

We sit for a few minutes, neither of us talking. I wish he could say more. I wish I could tell him about Ms. Stern. Maybe he'd tell me to go for it. But I can't risk it.

"Rayne." He leans in and looks me right in the eyes. "Your speech recognition is dropping. Your mom's right about that. She's also right that implants will most likely improve your recognition—possibly even get it to one hundred percent. For that reason, I understand where she's coming from."

The big lump in my throat has returned, clogging the whole darn thing. I can barely speak. I thought for sure he was on my side. "So do I, but I don't agree with her. And I should have a say. Thanks for seeing me."

Please let Ms. Stern be able to help me. She's my only hope now. Even if it means Mom and Dad hate me when this is all over.

CHAPTER 14

In the morning, I jump—practically to the ceiling—when there's a knock on my bedroom door.

Before I even say Come in, Mom opens it. "It's already eleven o'clock. I brought *** *** breakfast."

I wish I hadn't already put my hearing aids in—a dead giveaway that I was awake—but I can't remember a time Mom's ever brought me a full breakfast in bed. Maybe she feels bad about our fight the other night. Maybe she gets my point now, after I yelled like that. Maybe me not talking to my parents the last few days has helped them see how serious I am and made them change their minds.

I sit, and she puts the tray over my lap before joining me, sitting on the edge of the bed near my feet. "How *** *** feeling?"

The question doesn't actually make sense, and I

wonder if she's trying to trick me. It's not like I'm sick. "I'm fine. Why?"

"Just wondering *** you're still mad that we're taking *** to *** *** surgeon."

Of course I'm mad. I'm more than mad. I'm a-whole-lot-of-words-that-I'm-not-allowed-to-say kind of mad. But I can't give Mom a reason to think I contacted a lawyer.

"Rayne?" She studies my face.

"No, I'm not mad." Wait. Bad move. That's a dead giveaway. I have to still be upset, so she doesn't suspect. "I mean, yeah, I'm mad. But it's not like I can do anything about it. Right?"

"I wish *** see *** doing what's best for—"

"You!" I snap. "What's best for you."

"That's not true. *** act like *** making a rash decision. That we—"

"Please," I say. "Can we not have this same conversation over and over? You got your doctor appointment. You set the surgery. I don't want to keep talking about it."

She sighs, long and heavy. "I love you. I do. So does Dad." She stands and kisses the top of my head. "Bring *** dishes out when *** ***, okay?"

I don't answer, but as soon as she's gone, I unplug

my phone from the charger and FaceTime Colby. I'm so glad this exists, or I wouldn't be able to talk on the phone at all anymore. I guess if there's a good time to be going deaf, now is it. Technology is amazing, which is why I know the stem cell research will have a major breakthrough soon.

When Colby's face appears, he's rubbing his eyes as he rolls over. Of course he's still in bed too. "*** What's up? *** I didn't call *** back."

"Mom and Dad, that's what's up." I feel bad for waking him, but I need him. "You're not going to believe this. They already scheduled the surgery for me to have the implants. Without even telling me first. Without even meeting the doctor yet. Who does that?"

"*** *** *** ***," he says.

Even with the Bluetooth streaming his voice right into my aids, I need to read his lips to make sense of the words. "Flick on your light. I can't see your face."

He sits up in bed and pulls the cord on the window shade above him. Sunlight bursts into his dorm room. "Sorry. Yeah, but they can cancel it if you guys don't like the doctor once you meet ***."

"Wait! So you already knew about this?" I'm shaking my head, warp speed.

"Yeah, *** told me when I was home."

"And you didn't think to clue me in? You're supposed to be on my side. And I need that now more than ever. Before they can force some doctor to cut into my skull and ruin me forever."

"Come on. They're *** parents, not some strangers *** *** trying to hurt you."

I just . . . I can't even . . . I'm so . . . I don't know what I am. I'm a whole lot of things. Like a million and one things rolled together ready to burst into infinity. This is the ultimate betrayal. "I have to go." I reach to press the red button on the screen.

"Rayne, no!" He brings his phone closer to his face. "Come on. Let's talk about it."

"Talk about what? You should have told me. I'm guessing you agree with them too. That I need the implants."

He's quiet.

I'm stewing.

With each passing second, I stew more.

"Forget it," I say. "I'll see you later."

"Yes," he blurts.

"Yes, what?"

"*** implants. I think you need them. I'm sorry, but I do. Even Sierra agrees. I don't want *** to miss out on stuff like you have ***. Our inside jokes and watching movies and even regular conversations at dinner. *** struggle with things *** *** time. Don't *** want to be able to communicate *** us?"

My heart pings because that's exactly what I miss.

When I don't answer, he pushes more. "Don't *** want to be able to hear again?"

"Like a robot, if at all? No thanks!"

For the first time, it hits me that my hearing and my ability to communicate are two different things. They don't necessarily have to go together. Maybe I should learn sign language like Mr. Faro suggested. Like really learn. Then again, unless everyone I know also learns it, it would be useless.

Or maybe I'd be like the kids at Bayview. Maybe I could even go to Bayview. It would be better than the implants. I think.

For now, though, it's obvious that my best option is Dr. Brandt's study. And getting Ms. Stern to make that happen.

Colby says, "It won't *** that bad. I've looked it up. *** won't even hardly see the . . ." He snaps his fingers. "The receptor things on the side of *** head, whatever they're called, because *** your hair. And even if *** could, who cares as long as you can live like *** want to?"

"So you're saying you'd get them, if this were you?"

His mouth twists sideways as he exhales.

"That's what I thought!" I say.

"No, I *would* get them. It's just that, I get why *** concerned. I would be too, if it *** me, but because it's not, it's easier *** me to be objective."

"Nope, it's just easier to lie and pretend it's not a big deal." This time, I don't warn him before I hang up.

———

The invitation for Beth's party is on my nightstand. I toss it aside and focus on Ms. Stern—currently my only hope of getting to Dr. Brandt. Once I win my case, I won't have to get the implants, but I wonder if that means I only win against getting implants, or if it means I get to decide to do whatever I want about my ears—including stem cells. I'll have to ask Ms. Stern once she takes my case. I need her to take it. Because if I can do what I want, Mom will have to drive me to Orlando. Then I'll beg Dr. Brandt myself to let me into that study.

The invitation is staring at me. I know Jenika wasn't kidding when she said she'd drag me there. Though I have to prove to Mom and Dad that I haven't ditched my social life, I also know there's no way I'm going to Beth's. The last thing I want is to watch everyone swimming and having chicken fights and stuff while I sit on a lounge chair. Even if Troy is there. Maybe especially since he'll be there. Adam will most definitely take shots at me and my hearing if I don't get in, but if I do get in, well, I won't hear a thing. I don't want people feeling sorry for me because I can't simultaneously swim and hear.

I throw on shorts and a tank top over my bathing suit. I collect a towel, the invitation, and Mom's notebook from the Harvest Fest meeting. I head for the living room. Even in the daylight, this room's so dark. Mom and Dad really need to paint the walls for me.

Dad's reading a book and Mom's watching a show about haunted homes. For a second, it hits me how typical this seems. How when they're not with me, their life is the same as it's always been. I can't remember the last time we've just hung out without talking about my ears.

I show them the invitation. "I completely forgot about Beth's party today. Is it okay if I go?"

Mom gets all flustered. "What? Oh, I don't even *** a gift *** her."

"It's okay. I can give it to her later. She won't care."

Dad's wearing a huge smile. "*** to see *** getting out, pumpkin."

Internally, I want to roll my eyes. Externally, I smile. "Yep. Everyone's going. I can't wait."

Mom heads toward the kitchen, her back to me. "*** *** *** *** *** *** ***."

This time, I do roll my eyes, and Dad says, "She said she's going to get her keys."

Perfect. Just as I planned. I kiss Dad on the cheek and dart for the door.

Outside, I grab my bike from the garage, as Mom makes her way toward the car.

"Actually," I say, "I'm riding my bike to Jenika's, and we're going to ride to Beth's together."

"Oh." Mom pauses next to the car, door wide open. "I guess that's okay." She turns away from me to close it, but before she does, I snap a selfie of the two of us without her seeing.

I kiss her on the cheek. "See you later."

I grab my bike and wait for her to go back into the house. Before I pedal away, I text Jenika the photo of Mom and me near the car.

Me: *Sorry! Parents forcing me to spend day with them.*

Prob trying to make me forget about surgery. Did you see R-Jarrow's countdown today?

Jenika: *Yes! Two pink elephants. Def circus. Bummer! Sounds lame, but try to have fun.*

I send a thumbs-up emoji.

Jenika: *You better not be lying to me!!!!*

I don't reply. Instead, I stash my phone on one of the garage shelves. If Mom decides to track me, she'll just think I left my phone there by accident.

I set off for the library to spend the day writing a kick-butt donation letter for the Harvest Fest.

Mom keeps a lot of notebooks, and as luck would have it, I brought the wrong one. This one's full of notes about my ear stuff. Maybe that's a sign that I should spend this time learning even more about the surgery. If I don't hear from Ms. Stern soon, and Mom and Dad make me go to Dr. Olsen's on Friday, I have to have my argument ready for why CIs are one thousand percent not the answer for me. After I've drafted what I think the donation letter should say, I turn my attention to ear research. And try not to think about that last text from Jenika.

Lying feels pretty awful. Just like this whole last year. My Box of Shame is growing.

CHAPTER 15

On our way out of school the next day, I tell Mom that Mr. Grady asked to see me. She follows me to his classroom.

"Come on ***," he says. "Rayne, you're *** tremendous writer. I love *** *** played up *** students and our specific needs *** at school. Where'd *** come up *** that?"

Mom asks, "What did *** write about?"

"I don't know." I shrug. "I mean, my dad and brother are obsessed with sports. They watch them all the time when they're together. But I like when the games cut off and the commentators talk about *certain* players and tell their life stories. I always care about them more when I know the *why* part. So instead of just asking people for money, I thought I'd give examples, like how the drama kids can't have shows here because we don't have microphones, and since they have to do the shows at my dad's school and lots of kids don't have a way to get there, those kids can't be in the shows at all. Maybe people will read about that and want to give money."

Mom smiles. "That *** really something."

Mr. Grady's shaking his head. "Brilliant, truly. I *** no doubt *** letter will serve *** well."

"Thanks," I say.

Mom puts her arm around my shoulder as we walk out to the car.

———

It took a lot of begging, but our parents have agreed to let Jenika sleep over, even though it's a school night. R-Jarrow's dropping either a new single or a whole album tonight, and we can hardly wait another minute. Thankfully, we only have to wait six more.

We've pored over the clues from the last few weeks and decided that it's probably a single, but that the album will come in the next week or two. Today's clue was just one circus tent with the words *Singled out 9 • 13 Uncaged . . .*

Jenika points to the last clue. "The date *** a no

brainer, but 'singled out *** uncaged' . . . it could mean the single comes out tonight, *** it's called 'Uncaged.'"

"No." I grab a handful of popcorn and shove it in my mouth. "I bet the album's called *Uncaged*. Think about the circus clues."

"What *** there's no album for a while!"

"How do you know? Where are you reading that?"

"What?"

"That there's no album for a while?"

"If." She hugs me. "I said *if*. Sorry."

"Thank goodness." I look over the clues again. "This is maddening!"

"For sure." She refreshes her phone and checks the clock: 11:59 p.m.

My heart's flipping. "A new album would mean a new tour."

Jenika says, "Yes! We'll get tickets."

I know Dr. James said my hearing's hanging by a thread lately and concerts and loud places could make it worse, but for R-Jarrow, it would be worth the risk. "It's midnight. Go, go, go!" I bounce on the bed.

"*** my gosh, here we go." She refreshes again and sure enough, there's a new single with the album cover. "Uncaged" is the name of the song *and* the album, and the background is a circus tent with R-Jarrow next to two elephants whose chains are cut. All of it's framed in pastel colors, mostly pink.

For a second, we both just stare.

"It's so beautiful." I bounce on the bed again. "Play it."

"I'm working *** it." She yanks me beside her, and we sit as the music starts.

I close my eyes, soaking it all in as the music plays.

There are words. I know this because I hear them. But I also don't hear them. Or at least I can't understand them. I open my eyes, check Jenika's phone, and ask, "What's wrong with the song?"

Jenika shushes me and sways.

"Seriously." I take her phone and start the song over, but it sounds the same. A line about freedom. And something. But it's not clear.

Jenika's staring at me wide-eyed.

I hand her the phone. "Download it again." I turn up the volume on my aids.

She says nothing.

"Obviously something happened. It's all garbled."

She looks at her phone but doesn't delete or download a new version.

"Come on. You can't possibly tell me you heard the words."

She raises her eyes to mine.

"No. My ears aren't that bad. I just had them tested."

She plays an old R-Jarrow song, and I can hear it. Relief floods my bones. I sing along to every word.

Jenika hits pause. "Do *** hear the words, *** do *** just know them by heart?"

"Of course, I hear them."

She plays the old song again. And I listen. I hear the music. I can even feel it—the rhythm and all that—but when I focus, like really focus, the truth is, I can't understand the actual words she's singing. I've just memorized them. What the heck?

My breath catches. When did this happen? I try to reach for Jenika's shoulder, but my arm won't move, and I know, without even thinking, this is it. Everything's over. If I can never hear R-Jarrow again, I pretty much have nothing.

CHAPTER 16

No matter how much I try to avoid Troy, he doesn't give up. This morning, he's waiting outside my house with a cherry Pop-Tart. He knows it's my favorite kind, but I have zero appetite. Zero desire to say or do anything. Zero idea if I should even wait for Ms. Stern to reply. I mean, it's only been two days, if you don't count the weekend. But still. None of it matters. None. Not even Troy grabbing my hand and looping his fingers in mine.

I pull my hand back.

Jenika takes the Pop-Tart from me and shoves the corner of it in my mouth. "Say thank you, Ray."

I nearly choke as a piece of it tries to lodge itself permanently in my windpipe.

Troy faces me and looks ready to perform the Heimlich maneuver, but I put my hand up to stop him, as the chunk of half-chewed goodness springs from my mouth, barely missing him.

"Are *** okay?" he asks.

I don't answer, because I'm not okay, but it doesn't even matter anymore.

"I never realized a Pop-Tart could be so dangerous. *** should put *** warning on the box not to eat and walk at *** *** time." He takes my hand again, not embarrassed one bit that I almost hurled the thing right at him. I think back as far as I can and try to remember a time I've ever seen Troy embarrassed about anything.

Nada. Zip. Zilch. And for some reason, all of a sudden, this makes me angry.

I ask, "What's the most embarrassing thing that's ever happened to you?"

"Hmmm." He cocks his head sideways and scrunches his mouth. "That's *** *** question."

"Nothing ever bothers you, does it?"

"*** *** one time—okay, *** it *** last week actually—that I took my warm-up pants *** right before the swim meet. I could *** sworn I'd put my bathing suit ***, but turns out it *** just me standing *** in my underwear."

Jenika cracks up.

"Great." I fold my arms. "In front of everyone?"

"Well, yeah, I *** on the pool deck, but I'm not sure *** many people actually saw."

I probably would have run for the locker room and never, *ever* competed again. But not him. I know him. Still, I ask, "What did you do?"

"What could I ***? I just laughed and pulled my warm-ups back ***."

I knew it. Classic Troy.

He reaches for my hand again. "I'm glad I could give *** team a laugh before we raced. *** definitely loosened everyone up."

"Stop!" I yell.

He freezes. Jenika reaches for me, but I pull away.

I ask Troy, "How do you do that?"

"Do what?"

"Not care. How do you let stuff go without it bothering you, like what people say or think? It's not human."

"***, I couldn't change it, right? I mean, I didn't *** my racing trunks ***, and I couldn't make *** magically appear. So I laughed about *** instead."

"Okay, but you were embarrassed deep down, right? The laugh was just to cover that up." It had to be.

He shrugs. "Nope. *** stuff doesn't bother me. Everyone messes *** sometimes."

I let his words settle. "Maybe if something's an accident, but it's different with things you can't change." I definitely can't laugh off my hearing problem.

We're halfway to school, and Troy stops to face me. "What *** you thinking? You seem lost inside *** head."

I'm way more than lost. It's like the sidewalk's ended. There's nowhere else to go. "Some things can't be laughed off." I stare at my shoes and fight the eel that's stinging in my chest.

"*** *** *** *** *** ***."

"See." I toss my arms in the air. "How can I not be embarrassed that I don't have a clue what you just said to me, all because I wasn't looking at your face? If that's not embarrassing, I don't know what is."

"Why does it embarrass you?"

"What? Are you kidding?" I huff. "Because . . ." How do I even explain it? "Because there's something wrong with me!"

"That's not true," Jenika says.

"Look." Troy holds up his right palm. "My middle finger is shorter than both *** fingers *** each side of it."

"You don't get it!" I scream. "Your finger isn't a big deal. Most people wouldn't even know."

"I don't get why you think *** hearing loss is *** big deal."

I swear I could spit fire. "Because it *is*. Because people assume I'm not smart when I answer the wrong things. Or they think I'm mean because sometimes I don't answer at all, when I actually just didn't hear them. And it's a big deal because half the time I feel invisible—at parties, in school, even at dinner with my own family. And the few times I don't feel invisible all have to do with my not being able to hear, and those times, I wish I *was* invisible. There's no winning for me."

"Just because *** can't laugh it *** doesn't mean *** have to be embarrassed by it. It doesn't bother me that *** need *** little help hearing."

A little help? A little? He'd feel differently if he knew how bad it's going to get. Or that, if Mom and Dad have their way, I'll soon have mechanical ears in only twelve weeks. TWELVE WEEKS! I shudder.

"It doesn't bother me either!" Jenika says extra loudly.

This sets me off because she knows how horrible last night was for me. The reality of it all. "It's easy to say you wouldn't be embarrassed by this, because you both hear fine, so you don't know. You can't possibly get it."

They stare at me.

"And I'm getting tired of you saying it's no big deal, because it's a huge deal. Do you even know what I'll look like with the implants?"

They still say nothing.

"Do you?" I pull papers from my backpack. "Let me show you." I shove the pictures at them. "See? They're ginormous. I'll look like a freak. There's no hiding those knobs unless I wear a ski cap every single day."

Troy stares at the printout. "I *** no idea they'd look like that."

And suddenly, I wish he hadn't said anything at all. Because all this time, I knew if he actually knew what was going on, there was no way he'd like me. I can't stay here one more minute. My chest is squeezing my heart. My head's spinning.

Jenika stares at me with the *I-feel-sorry-for-you* face. I hate it. Hate it so much!

So I turn and run.

No clue where I'm going, other than away from school. I want to run all the way to the beach. I wish

I could. I wish I knew the way and my legs could last that long. And that no bad people would see me on the way—a kid walking alone. No, the beach is out. I keep walking, though. Maybe I should go to the park. But Mom basically brainwashed me as a kid with stranger-danger warnings, and I can't bring myself to go.

I stop in the middle of the road and throw my backpack to the ground. I can't even skip school properly. I almost yell, but I catch myself because the last thing I need is someone seeing me. Instead, I kick my backpack before picking it up and heading home.

I jump in bed and snuggle with Lucky. She's probably the only one in the whole world who truly doesn't care that I'll soon be deaf.

———

Of course, Mom freaked when she realized I'd cut school yesterday, so this morning she makes me ride with her to guarantee I'll show up. Which is okay because all I did yesterday was jump every time a car drove down the street. That and refresh my email over and over hoping Ms. Stern would reply. It's all so frustrating. So were the million texts from Jenika asking if I'm okay.

Troy only sent one. I didn't answer.

Eventually I looked up the lyrics to "Unchained" and wrote them in my notebook. Hoping to memorize them. What if music does sound better, normal, with implants? Would it be worth getting them then?

I do a search for this. The first result that pops up is an article from a place called Tech Talk. It says: *While cochlear implants (CI) may improve speech perception for those with profound hearing loss, many CI users aren't able to enjoy music due to the fact that CIs don't transfer pitches well and sound is compromised—leaving it flat for listeners. Implantees have reported that much of what they used to love, in regard to music, is now absent.*

I cannot win. This thing that Mom and Dad swear will make my life better, will actually ruin music for me even more. I couldn't figure out R-Jarrow's lyrics the other night, but I at least I still heard the music. How can they take that away from me? Why can't one single freaking good thing come from this entire mess?

Everything's foggy. I'm moving and doing what I have to, but it feels kind of like watching myself from far away. It's me, but it's not me. Nothing really matters now anyway.

We get to school super early since Mom has a parent conference before classes. I head to the media center to finish my makeup work. When I finally check the time on my phone, I cringe. My plan was to leave way before the warning bell so I could avoid Troy, Jenika, and the rest of the group when they gather in the hall, but I'm obviously too late. They're standing in our usual spot outside the library when I push through the door.

"Hey!" Jenika grabs my arm and pulls me into the circle. There are still four minutes before homeroom starts, so I can't even use that as an excuse to leave.

Troy throws me a tight-lipped smile, like he has to because I'm there, but I can tell he's uncomfortable. He's probably still grossed out by the pictures of the implants. I don't blame him, but all I want is to escape this hallway. Now.

Isabelle says, "We *** *** talking *** *** *** *** together to go to Halloween *** *** in Orlando *** *** *** weeks. *** definitely ***, right? You've *** loved a *** scare."

I toss the words I managed to hear around in my head, jigsaw-puzzling them together, all while trying my best to ignore Troy. My cheeks grow hot as everyone looks at me. Waiting for me to respond. There was definitely a question in there somewhere.

I fake a laugh. "Yeah, Halloween's great. My favorite holiday." It isn't. I don't know why I even said that.

Jenika loops her arm in mine and is careful to enunciate her words without yelling. "So of course, she'll go with us to Halloween Horror Nights. I'm sure my mom will drive."

"Yep. Sounds great." Crowds = noise. Darkness = zero lip reading. Not a chance I'll go. Still, I squeeze Jenika's arm to thank her and turn to leave as quickly as possible. Part of me hopes Troy will follow. He doesn't, though, and a little piece of my heart tears.

———

Lately, I've been slipping my SurfCon onto the podium before anyone gets into class, so Mr. Walsh doesn't have to ask me for it in front of everyone. I even told him that he doesn't have to actually wear it—that because it's close to him, it works fine. Which isn't a lie, as long as he stays up front. It's working with all my teachers.

After announcements and attendance, Mr. Walsh says, "Now that we've covered *** *** Newton's Laws, *** *** look over to *** lab tables, you'll see I've set fourteen stations." He points to the side of the room. "Each station has an activity which correlates with one *** Newton's three laws. You will have *** partner —" Even with the SurfCon, I'm still missing a few words today.

Immediately everyone stops listening and yells to others around the room, teaming up before he can go any further.

Mr. Walsh whistles, and it's like a train blaring directly into my ears. I jump sky high.

He yells, "Settle down!" When everyone does, he finishes. "This *** for *** grade. You and your partner will rotate through each of *** experiments, changing stations when I tell you to, *** you will document *** results. Later we will have *** all-class discussion, which will *** be worth some *** your grade. Understand?"

I have no idea if I understand. My ears are ringing loudly from the whistle, making me dizzy.

There are mumbles around the room.

"***, partners." He points to the first desk in the first row. "*** will count one. We'll go around till we hit fourteen, then *** next person will begin *** one again. So *** twenty-eight of you, it should work out *** two at each station."

I rub my temples to dull the pain and count each person in my own head, because I can't hear them calling out their numbers. When Mr. Walsh points to me, I say, "Thirteen." That's always been my lucky number. I look to see who the second-to-last person is—knowing it will be my partner—and my stomach flops.

Adam.

As if this day wasn't already bad enough.

CHAPTER 17

Station thirteen's activity demonstrates Newton's Third Law of Motion—that every action has an equal and opposite reaction. Adam gets there before me, since it's practically next to his desk. He has the directions in hand and makes no effort to show me when I approach the lab table.

To be honest, I couldn't care less about this. About the lab. About school. Not even about Troy. But if I'm going to have any hope of proving Mom wrong in court, I have to keep my grades up. I'll have to show the judge Mom's wrong about my whole life changing for the worse just because of my broken ears.

My phone vibrates with a message from our student government's Don't Forget app. *Sponsor letters for the Harvest Fest are due tomorrow.*

I have no clue what it's about. I already wrote a letter, which I thought was for sponsors, but maybe it was for donations only. Since I grabbed the wrong notebook the other day, I never figured out everything Mr. Grady said at the meeting. Maybe I'll work on another letter now, since Adam obviously wants to do this lab alone.

Suddenly, he straightens.

"Rayne," Mr. Walsh practically yells. "I'm talking *** ***."

A good portion of the class stops and stares.

He says, "I asked what's going *** here." He points to the phone in my hand. "Are *** looking to get *** detention, young lady?"

I could say I'm researching the directions to this lab online since Adam won't share with me, but there's no point in getting him in trouble, even though he's a pain, and I'm certainly not going to mention my hearing aids in front of everyone. "No, I just needed to make sure the volume was off. I forgot to do that before class started."

Mr. Walsh says, "First warning. Don't make me *** over here again."

I nod, but just as I'm about to slip the phone into my backpack, it vibrates again. An email. My palms sweat. I have to look. With Mr. Walsh safely walking toward the other side of the room, I check it.

```
Dear Ms. Campbell,

Thank you for contacting me. Sorry
for the delay in my reply. I've been
trying diligently to find an avenue
in which to proceed with your unique
case. After discussing this with my
colleagues and investigating further,
I'm afraid I'm not able to take you on
as a client. Your age has proven to be
the main hurdle holding us back, since
courts won't typically consider medical
emancipation for anyone younger than
the age of sixteen. I do wish I had
better news, as I'm intrigued by your
circumstances. I'm truly so very sorry.

Best regards,
M.A. Stern
```

I might vomit. Not like in the exaggerating kind
of way, but for real.

The phone's heavy in my hand.

Adam's doing something with the marbles, who
knows what—my head's replaying Ms. Stern's email.

Suddenly there's a low crashing sound. The marbles shoot in opposite directions.

It's hypnotic to watch.

The tin pan. My eyes lock on it.

In my head, I see a judge. I'm in front of him. He asks me if I'm sure about what I'm doing. I nod without looking at my parents behind me. He bangs his gavel, surely about to tell me I've won the case, but all of a sudden, his gavel explodes into music notes I can't even hear.

I jump and knock the pan off the table.

Mr. Walsh comes over again. "Adam?"

Adam spews words to Mr. Walsh. Apologies? I don't know.

I can barely hear. The room's spinning.

I feel . . . like . . .

Nothing.

Because I am. And because everything is.

Nothing.

Jenika's patting my back. "Come ***, Ray. Adam, tell Mr. Walsh it was *** accident."

I look toward Mr. Walsh, but instead, behind him, I see Troy. He's laughing with the guys at his table, while holding two paper cups on either side of his head.

Like Frankenstein. Like implants.

My skin prickles like the sting of a thousand jellyfish.

Troy sees me and stops mid-laugh, lowering the cups.

I knew it. I knew he'd change his mind about liking me once he actually saw the implants and knew how bad things were really going to get. But I never, ever thought he'd actually make fun of me.

There's an octopus clutching me.

I'm losing air.

I grab my things and run for the door.

———

I wander the hallway. And wander more. Mr. Faro's door's next to me. I push it open. Empty. I lock it behind me, slide down the cold wall, and ball up on the cement floor—my hearing aids shrieking from the nearness. I take them both out and place them in front of me. Small, mechanical miracles.

For some.

Just not for me.

I close my eyes and wonder, *What's the sign for broken?*

Someone's shaking me furiously.

"What? What?" I look around, for a moment forgetting I'm in Mr. Faro's storage room.

He's yelling, but I can't understand him. Behind him is . . . what . . . a firefighter?

I point to my ears, then search the floor for my aids. I grab both of them but can only find one of the batteries, so I put it in the aid of my better ear.

Mr. Faro looks both panicked and relieved. "Didn't *** hear *** fire alarm?"

I shake my head. "Is there a fire?"

"Thankfully, no. Ms. Belmont burned pizzas *** *** cafeteria, but *** smoke set *** *** alarm."

"Why is the firefighter here?"

The firefighter answers, "We come anytime *** alarm goes ***. Do *** know how lucky you *** that *** *** nothing?"

I nod, but honestly, I still just feel numb.

Mom pushes past the firefighter and Mr. Faro. "Rayne, *** my gosh. Rayne!" She inspects every inch of me and then wraps me in her arms. She pulls away again. "Do *** have any idea how worried I was when *** didn't show up *** *** field

*** your class? Mr. Walsh told me *** walked out of *** lab without permission. My goodness, what *** going on *** ***? Didn't *** hear *** alarm?"

"I took my aids out. I was asleep."

"Don't ever, *ever* *** that again." She hugs me again, but my arms are heavy, and I don't hug her back. When her tears seep into my hair, I pull away, so all her worry can't drip into my aid.

CHAPTER 18

Dad's home from work early. When he walks through the front door, he scoops me into his arms for so long I wonder if he'll let go before tomorrow. I can feel his breathing finally slow, and he sets me down.

I've never seen him cry before, and his red, puffy eyes scare me more than I want to admit. I mean, I know he cares about me. I never doubted that, but it's nice to be reminded of just how much since we've been fighting all the time lately.

He inspects my face and cups it in his hands. "I'd be nothing *** anything ever happened to ***."

"Dad." I hug him again. "I'm fine. I promise."

"No!" He shakes his head. "No, *** not. And I don't mean it *** a bad way, but you're not fine. This hearing loss *** a safety hazard. I'm so sorry, pumpkin, *** this *** changes everything. We need *** do something about *** ears as soon as possible."

"Please, Dad." I wipe at my eyes. "No." But it barely comes out as a whisper. I'm so tired. Of trying and getting nowhere. Of not being heard. I give up. Surrender. Wave the flag.

It's clear that implants are my destiny as long as I'm living under this roof.

Tomorrow's my meeting with Dr. Olsen, and I don't want Mom doing all the talking or covering up important information that I should know. Or worse, sprinkling heaps of sugar on the conversation when I ask about the surgery and recovery process and losing my normal hearing and music sounding awful, because honestly, those are the things that terrify me most. Thinking about them is what makes me want to escape to Delphinus forever.

But I really, really want to be less afraid. Little kids have done this surgery; I should have nothing to worry about. On my laptop, I search for *cochlear implant surgery*. I hate that images are always the first thing to pop up when you search for stuff. Especially now. Because the staples on this first girl's head look like train tracks laid by someone who just got off a fast-spinning merry-go-round. Before I can scroll down, the next picture catches my eye. Ohmygosh, ohmygosh. I grip my laptop. The photo shows the implant actually being put inside the head. Seriously, the skin is pulled back and the head's wide open. I vomit-burp in my mouth and toss my computer across the bed. Lucky jumps.

I stand. And pace. My arms stiffen as I try to shake them out. Cold. So cold. I climb in bed. Under the covers. I pull Lucky up to my neck. But I can't stop shaking.

I can't do it.

I can't.

Not the surgery. None of it. But what other options do I have?

I pretend to sleep the whole hour and a half it takes to get to Dade University in Miami, but really in my head, I'm going over the things the doctor will probably say in favor of the implants and rehearsing my responses.

I get a text from Jenika.

Jenika: *Good luck. Love you no matter what, but if you have to get them, maybe you'll hear R-Jarrow again? Stay sunny, girl!*

My stomach drops as I'm reminded that the opposite is true.

Mom, Dad, and I spend another hour and fifteen minutes in the waiting room and then another forty-five in the private room. Normally, Mom would make a scene about this, but not today. Her smile is plastered on like a clown's. Dad spends his time on the iPad researching safety measures. At one point, he tells Mom he's stepping outside to call our local fire department to come inspect our house and help set up a fire alarm for deaf people. He shows me a picture of a mat thing that will go under my pillow and shake me awake in an emergency. I've become a hazard.

Finally, Dr. Olsen comes in wearing a white coat and a bright orange tie. He looks like he's old enough to be my grandfather, and when he smiles, he seems like he's probably going to be really nice. I look away. I have to stay focused. Remember the photos. Remember no music again. I can't give in.

He reaches out to shake my hand, speaking very clearly, which I'm sure is for me. "Nice to finally meet you, Rayne."

I cross my arms over my chest and say nothing.

Dad firmly plants his arm in the middle of my back. "Rayne!"

I force my hand out to shake the doctor's, but I

definitely don't say it's nice to meet him too. That would be a lie.

Mom brushes hair from her eyes. "*** sorry, Dr. Olsen. This has *** *** very tough *** Rayne."

"Yep," I add. "But it's been really easy for my parents."

Mom apologizes again, and Dad shakes his head at me.

Dr. Olsen sits on his stool and thankfully doesn't ask me to sit on the table for an exam. He says, "Rayne, I know this can be quite scary, but I assure you, I'm here to answer any questions you have."

"Great." I lean forward. "Have you ever had any other patients whose parents forced them to have the implants, or am I your first?"

Dr. Olsen's eyes grow bigger, and he takes a breath.

Dad moves his face near mine. "That's enough."

I glare at him.

Dr. Olsen looks like he's about to say something to me, but he turns toward Mom instead. "So now that the insurance has approved Rayne for implants based on her most recent hearing tests, we'll need to schedule a chest x-ray and an MRI as soon as possible."

I ask, "Don't you also have to schedule me for a psychological exam?"

"That's correct," he says. "You've been doing your homework."

I nod. "I have. And you should probably know that I have a lot of mental health problems. I'm pretty sure I won't pass. So what happens then?"

Dad grabs me by my elbow and herds me toward the door. "Excuse ***. We'll be right back."

Outside, I think he's going to yell at me, but instead, he gives me a hug and says right into my ear, "I know this is hard for you. And maybe you don't believe it, but this is the hardest thing I've ever had to do too. Ever. The fire alarm was a wake-up call. I wish we hadn't come to this point, but here we are. And I worry that you're going to hate me forever. But I also know this is right. Now please go in there and just listen."

I don't move. If I do, I'll crumble.

"Rayne, I love you. So much. Please know that."

But I shake my head. Because if he loved me, he wouldn't make me do this.

Dr. Olsen doesn't stop talking when we walk back in. He just keeps on going, focusing on Mom and not me. He's not saying a single thing I don't already know, thanks to my research, and the way he's pretending this is all so fabulous is making me more and more furious. I try—like really, really try—to keep my thoughts inside, but every word, every lie gnaws at my belly.

Finally, I ask, "And what happens if the surgery fails?"

He answers, "Oh, we're very good here at DU. We have a success rate of ninety-eight percent."

"But what if I'm in the two percent? What if my body rejects the implant, or it malfunctions, or my whole head gets an infection? What happens then?"

"Well, we could always do a revision surgery."

"Yeah, put me through this whole thing again and hope it works better the second time. Which also isn't guaranteed."

Dr. Olsen stands. "How about I give you all a minute."

"Wait," I say. "Let me ask you one question first."

"Sure. Anything."

"You're a science guy, right?"

He nods.

"Then tell me why I shouldn't wait for stem cells to fix my hearing."

He straightens, like he's confident in this answer. "We don't do stem cell research here. We do implants."

"Exactly." I toss my hands up. "Which is why

you recommend the implants. But if you guys were as smart as the doctors at Harvard or Stanford, and you knew all about stem cells, I bet you'd tell me to wait."

Mom stands, blocks me from view, and reaches for Dr. Olsen's hand. "I *** so, *** sorry. I *** never seen *** like ***. Please forgive ***, but I think it's best *** we leave *** ***. I'll be *** touch very *** to follow up *** what we need to *** to proceed."

He leans past Mom, looks at me, and says, "It really is nice to meet you, Rayne. I'm impressed by how well prepared you were today. To answer your earlier question, you are the first child I've had who has refused the implants. But I promise, if you think about the alternative, you might change your mind. CIs have the potential to restore your hearing one hundred percent in certain situations. I'd be happy to put you in touch with kids your age who have had the surgery and are quite thankful for it. But only if you want."

With that, he walks out the door. Before I can tell him thanks but no thanks. Nothing's going to change my mind.

CHAPTER 19

The ride home from Miami is as quiet as the ride down, and even though it's Friday, which means football, I'm definitely not going to the game. I'm not even sure if Mom and Dad will, but I hope they do.

I'm in the kitchen grabbing a can of Dr. Pepper when an eerie witch's laugh and high-pitched cackling pierce my ears. As much as I'm getting used to most things about the Bluetooth hearing aids, it still freaks me out every time the high-tech doorbell rings in my ears. Especially since Dad's corny about it, always changing the ring. I wasn't expecting this one—though I should have been, with Halloween coming.

From the kitchen, I see Dad let a guy in.

"Who's that?" I ask.

Mom pulls a box of pasta from the cabinet. She sighs, and I can tell she doesn't really want to answer. Probably because of the way I talked to Dr. Olsen, which I totally wouldn't have had to do if she hadn't forced me to go. She hasn't said a word to me since we left Miami. Finally, she answers, "*** were right. We *** have a leak in the roof and *** water damage."

I slap my thigh. "Totally called that." I swear my sense of smell has gotten stronger as my hearing's gotten worse.

She shakes her head. "Luckily, it seems we *** patch it instead *** replacing *** *** thing, which is a blessing because we've spent a *** *** *** savings on *** hearing aids *** *** last year, *** we can't afford *** *** new roof right ***. *** guy's inspecting *** mold. Hopefully *** *** none *** we *** simply repaint *** ceiling. A much cheaper option." She sits heavily, like she's got all this weight on her.

"If we're hurting for money so badly, why are you paying for me to have surgery?"

She wipes her hands on a dishtowel and tosses it on the counter. "Remember? *** found out insurance will cover ***."

"So wait." I process everything. "How much were the hearing aids?"

"Over *** thousand ***."

"Nine thousand?" I gulp.

"No, five. I said, five thousand. Sorry."

Still . . . "Insurance didn't cover those?"

She shakes her head. "Criminal, right? It's not like hearing aids *** cosmetic."

I get it now. "Is that one of the reasons you're doing this?" I can see it in my head so clearly, and my voice gets louder. "The insurance won't pay for my hearing aids, and maybe they never will for the rest of my life. That will be a whole lot of money every time I need new ones. But insurance pays for implants. Then you guys don't have to worry about money anymore."

Dad shoots me a look from the living room, but I don't care. This makes sense.

"You guys complain about money all the time, but this option . . ." I point wildly at my ears. "Me having surgery is free. Is that why you're forcing me to do it? Is that why it doesn't matter that I've begged you a million times not to?"

Dad leaves the repairman and joins us in the kitchen. "Stop it. No matter what, you do not talk to us like that."

"What are you going to do? Ground me? Who

cares? There's not much you can do except make me get the implants."

And I won't let you.

The holes in Dad's nose are flaring as fast as my heart's beating. He inhales through gritted teeth and says, "Give me your phone, and go to your room."

I slap my phone into his open hand, happy to go to my room. It's the only place I want to go, actually. Mom's wiping tears from her cheeks. She doesn't care about my tears, though. I can't care about hers.

———

Other than taking Lucky for a few walks, because my parents force me to, I don't leave my room all day Saturday, and not having my phone means I don't have to feel bad about not texting Jenika. Or realizing that Troy probably isn't texting me anymore.

I go to the NIDCD website and search for other studies like the Orlando one. Since Mom called Dr. Brandt, maybe she'll at least consider one of these too. My notebook's full of doctor names and trials, and I'm especially hopeful about a stem cell study that's already working at Whitley University. It uses a virus cell, since that travels fastest in the body. Once

Mom and Dad read this and see that this treatment already exists, that it's not five hundred years away, maybe they'll change their minds.

I'm heading to the printer when I pass the living room. Mom's got her keys and her purse.

Dad's tucking his wallet into the pocket of his jeans. "Perfect timing. Let's go for a ride."

"Where?" I'm still mad at them and don't want to be with them at all. Plus, I have a lot to organize before I present my case about the stem cells.

Or maybe today's my day. My chance.

"We're *** to grab lunch *** run errands," he says.

I look toward the printer. "Okay, but I need a few minutes first." I grab the papers and walk to my room. I scan the documents quickly, make mental notes of the most important points, take a deep breath, and head to the car.

We pull up in front of a hotel, and as we get out of the car, I ask, "Are we eating here?"

Dad looks at Mom, questioning.

She nods. "There's food at *** event."

"Event?" I ask.

Mom sighs. Something about it scares me. I think it's because she looks a lot more like Grandma lately.

Mom hardly ever wore makeup until recently, but now it seems like she has it on every day. Maybe she's trying to cover the darkness under her eyes, but it doesn't really work. "Because we feel *** deserve *** know everything *** can, *** here *** attend *** cochlear implant support group."

"What? You lied to me?"

"Rayne." She cups my face. "Today's nothing more than *** meeting *** people. It's not fair that *** so against *** implants without doing *** part to find out everything *** can about ***."

"How can you say that? I've researched them a thousand times."

Dad bends down. "What are you so afraid of? Try explaining it *** us so we can explore those fears *** get better answers. For all of us."

I choke back tears. People are coming and going from the lobby. Some are staring at us, which I hate more than anything. I will not lose it right here. Publicly. I won't. So I can't answer him.

Definitely, I wish the implants weren't so big, but it's way more than that. I'm afraid of the surgery and all the things that could go wrong. I'm afraid of the implants not working once they're in. Of being in that two percent and losing what hearing I have left, all for nothing. And of having nowhere to go from there. I can still function now, but if the implants don't work for me, my usual life would be over. Mom's always told us to appreciate what we have. That it's greedy to ask for more. I swear she's a hypocrite. Her whole *the grass is greener where you water it and not on the other side of the fence* is obviously a bunch of bull.

A girl walks past us. She's holding hands with a boy. Both look like they're in high school, and for a minute I wonder if they know Dad, but they keep walking—into the lobby. When they're past us, I see the girl's implants under her ponytail. She's blinged those things out with aqua sequined somethings . . . maybe stickers? The color looks awesome with her dark hair. Seriously, she wasn't even trying to hide them. And her boyfriend didn't care either—he's not holding cups on his head making fun of her.

"Fine," I say. "I'll go in, but at least with Dr. Olsen you didn't lie to me about where we were going."

Mom nods. "*** right. I'm sorry. Thank you for going inside." She leads the way.

Dad waits for me, and I wonder if he thinks I'll bolt. As much as I'm considering it, I want to meet that girl with the aqua implants, so I go. Prepared to ask a million questions.

The room is big, but there are only about fifteen people inside. Most are adults, probably parents. Besides the girl and her boyfriend, I only count three other kids. All of them have implants.

Mom and Dad have no problem introducing themselves to everyone. I hang back and just watch. Eventually, the girl with the aqua implants comes over. She's alone. "Hey. I'm Maddie."

"I'm Rayne." I can't help but stare at her ears. The processor things are a lot like my hearing aids, hanging over her ears. But while mine go into my ear, hers hang down the back side and then connect to a round piece on the side of her head with a cord-thingy. Mostly, I'm surprised they're not as big in person as they always look on the internet. But they're not invisible.

She obviously sees me staring. "Do *** decorate *** too?"

My hair is down, so she must assume I have implants. "Oh, I just wear hearing aids. But yours are really pretty."

"Thanks. I love showing *** off."

"For real?" It's good to know that she speaks just

like me, even with implants. I wasn't sure how that would work. I've seen deaf people on social media who can't talk at all, or talk like they have food in their mouths, but obviously it's not like that for everyone. I probably shouldn't have assumed. And I suddenly wonder why I think this way at all—like my way of speaking is normal and other ways aren't.

"Yeah. Way cooler *** Wonder Woman's powers, don't *** think?"

Definitely not, but I don't tell her that. "Very cool. How long have you had them?"

"Four years." She pops a piece of cheese in her mouth.

"And you go to school?"

She nods.

"So when you're at school, can you, like, hear the announcements and stuff over the intercom?"

She nods again.

"Clearly or like you can just hear them talking but you don't know what they're actually saying?"

"It's perfectly clear. *** wasn't before, when I had hearing aids. I wish I had done *** implants sooner."

I look to see where Mom is. Surely, she's paying this girl money to say the right things to me. But Mom's chatting away with a lady who's holding a baby. That baby has implants too. A baby! Shouldn't that mom have waited till the kid was old enough to decide? Why do parents do that—make decisions and tell us it's for the best? Like they're smarter and only their opinions matter.

"*** okay?" asks Maddie.

"Yeah." I shake my head. "Yeah. So what made you decide to get them? Did your parents force you?"

"No, why would ***?" She looks at me like it's the weirdest question ever. "I wanted *** sooner, but *** insurance wouldn't cover it. We had to fight with them *** *** while."

"Oh, gotcha. Um, what about music? Can you hear it like you used to?" Please, please, please say yes.

"Honestly, at first, not at all. But it was the same with speech. Even though I can hear almost perfectly now, in talking and with some lyrics, I still don't really hear music clearly, like melodies or things like that."

My face falls. Tears sting behind my eyes.

"Hey." She puts her hand on my shoulder for a second, then lets it drop. "I promise you, it's still all worth it. It's changed my world. Before, without my hearing aids, I had zero percent word recognition."

"You couldn't hear anything?"

"Well, with my hearing aids I was at about eight percent, but nothing *** *** clear."

"Same here. At least for things not being clear." But I'm not even close to only eight. According to Dr. James, I'm at like twenty-three percent. "My aids work mostly well."

"*** lucky. They did for me too. For a while. But when it's time to get the implants, *** know *** sure. *** want them."

That! Yes! "That's exactly what I keep telling my parents. It's not time yet. Not now." If ever.

"And?"

"They won't listen to me."

"That's tough. But *** it's because *** want *** to be able to hear better. The implants definitely *** that."

"For some people. But not for everyone."

"True. But that's rare. Look, it's *** kinds of scary. Don't search stuff *** *** internet because *** pictures will freak *** the heck out."

"Too late for that."

"I promise, it's not as bad *** it seems. But *** have to be ready. *** be committed because *** a lot of work to *** after. *** don't just magically hear again. *** have to do homework and stuff, like a couple of hours a day. Retrain *** brain to under-stand speech. So if *** not ready for that, *** should probably wait."

That's exactly what I want. To wait. "Yeah, well, it was nice to meet you."

"*** too. Here, give me your number." She hands me her phone, and I type my number. "I'll text *** now, and you can reach me whenever *** want. Okay?"

"Sure. Thanks. But why are you even here?"

"I had to fight a long time to get *** implants, *** I vowed if I ever got approved, I'd help others do *** same, so I come to these whenever I can. Text me if *** have questions. Okay?"

"Definitely." In a few years. If I go fully deaf. But not before then.

Still, it's cool that she loves her implants. And that her parents didn't force her to get them.

When I'm at Dr. James's office (minus the Box of Shame) and even at Jenika's, no one judges me or expects me to be different than how I am. No one acts like my ears are a disappointment, or a problem to be solved, or a tragedy to overcome. That's all I want. To just live like me. However that is. Whether I'm deaf or hearing. I just want Mom and Dad to treat me like me.

I've replayed my conversation with that girl Maddie over and over in my head since we left the hotel. Another thing that keeps replaying—even though I'm trying a thousand ways to make it go away because I can't get past the photos—is Dr. Olsen telling me I could possibly hear one hundred percent again.

Possibly.

But possibly not.

It's weird that one word fills me with both hope and fear. The part of me that wants to feel hopeful about my life again, the part that wonders if I can someday be like Maddie, leads me to a hearing loss message board. I've been scrolling for hours and have learned a lot, but still, I want to ask my own questions. I want answers.

Finally, I make an account so I can post in the cochlear implant thread. I write, *Poll: are you happy you got implants or not?* It only takes a minute for the replies to start popping up.

The first twenty-six answers are overly happy yeses. People say they're happy to hear again. Some wish they had done it sooner. Maybe I'm making a big deal out of nothing. Maybe some of the information I found before was old. Maybe technology and doctors are better now, and patients no longer bleed out their ears afterward. And it's not like I'd be awake for the surgery or anything.

The first negative comment shows up. The person says I can contact him by private message on the site if I want specifics. Yes, I do. For sure.

Ben tells me he's nineteen, he got his implants two years ago, and it went horribly wrong.

R-girl: *Thanks for answering. What happened?*

Ben: *No problem. So I was hearing originally, but my speech recognition was only like 20%. Still, I sorta got along okay with hearing aids. But the idea of CIs sounded awesome. The doctors and audiologists gave me lots of hope, so I did bilateral—both ears at once. Four weeks after surgery was activation day, and I was stoked. But when they turned them on, I couldn't hear any speech, just mind-numbing noise. Nonstop. All day. Even after mappings and speech audio therapy, nothing got better. So after 15 months, they did a repair surgery, explanted and then implanted a whole new system, and I ended up with massive scar tissue in my head and still just noise. All noise.*

I don't even know how to reply. "I'm sorry" sounds wrong.

R-girl: *Oh, wow.*

Ben: *Yeah, I mean, I guess I'm glad I tried because I would never have known otherwise, and I didn't have much to lose anyway, since my hearing was almost non-existent, but still, I had so much hope. Expectations suck. You know?*

R-girl: *Yeah, I get that.*

Mom and Dad really need to read this. They need to get rid of their expectations.

R-girl: *Aren't you angry?*

Ben: *Nah, I've made peace with it. I still lip read and use captioning. I'll probably learn sign. I was really depressed, even before the implants, but I can't live my whole life that way. Therapy's been helping me out of that funk.*

R-girl: *I'm glad you're okay.*

Ben: *I'd be okay if the ringing and noises would just stop. It's there even when I take my processor off. I'm hoping someone can fix that.*

R-girl: *Wait, so you still wear the processor even though you can't hear words?*

Ben: *Yeah, I'm an optimist, I guess. Maybe someday they'll just magically start working for me. But there are days I want to rip the implant out on my own. I miss my quiet life, but then I do my breathing and try to remind myself it could be way worse.*

Honestly, I'm not sure what could be worse. I already have ringing without my aids, and I've read for some people that part gets even more intense with implants. That sounds unbearable to me.

R-girl: *Thank you so much for talking to me. I hope my parents will read your story and not make me get the implants.*

Ben: *Yeah, man, I mean, maybe they'd work, but if they don't, it's brutal. With 20/20 hindsight, I wish I'd never done anything. Keep me posted.*

R-girl: *Okay. Thanks.*

I feel bad for the guy, but I'm also kind of shocked that he's so chill about how everything turned out. I know he mentioned being depressed, but he also said he was glad things weren't worse. How? How does he do that? Just accept it?

And would he actually prefer being fully, permanently deaf? I want to know, because more than anything, I want to be okay with myself. And if going deaf is my only alternative to CIs, then maybe . . .

But what's the use of thinking like that? Mom and Dad will always see me as broken.

For now, I just need to focus on convincing them that the CIs aren't worth the risk. This conversation with Ben is the proof I need. The story Mom never wanted to hear or believe. This might save me.

Mom pats the oversized comfy chair in the living room. "Come here."

I open the blinds before I sit, and sunlight streams in. I'm glad they asked to talk. I have the message board conversation with Ben printed out and ready.

Mom's sitting on the identical chair across from mine and Dad's on the couch.

Mom puts her hair up in a clip. "That girl Maddie *** *** lot *** nice things about ***. Did *** get good information *** ***?"

"She likes her implants. That's great. But she was way worse off hearing-wise when she got her implants than I am. She even said I'd know when the time is right."

"I agree, but *** dad *** I are certain now is *** time," Mom says.

Dad adds, "We've researched for months. Months. We want to be up front *** you and tell you we've decided to move forward *** *** surgery in December."

"But wait," I say. "I have new information."

Dad says, "We've been through *** already. You don't think we're listening to ***, but your mom called Dr. Brandt . . ."

I say, "There are a lot more things being done than that one experiment. Did you know there's a study at Whitley University near Boston?" I grab my notebook, holding a page for them to see. "Right here. It says they're using a virus cell to implant the part of your own missing genetic code to fix your ears. Like whatever part of your code is missing, they only put that in the cell, and it goes to your ear and drops it off. Then your ear hairs can grow on their own. It's already working on monkeys."

They're both shaking their heads.

"I'm sure I'm not explaining it right. It was complicated when I read it, but it won't be long before this is an option for people."

"You are not a monkey!" Mom yells. "We've been through ***. Your hearing loss might have been caused by this very type *** thing!"

"Okay, well, if you really don't want to put me at risk, then answer me honestly. Promise?"

They both nod.

"Out loud."

"We promise," they both say.

"You keep telling me about these implant kids and how well the CIs have turned out for them."

"Yes," Mom says. "We've talked to lots ***

parents in *** same situation. Not one *** them regrets *** choice for *** implants."

I slap my legs. "Of course they don't regret it. They're like you. But here's my question, and you promised to be honest. Have you even tried talking to someone who thinks the implants were a mistake?"

Mom starts to speak but stops.

Dad looks at me, but he can't answer either.

"Exactly! See . . ." I hand them the printout of my conversation with Ben. "Read it. He regrets it. It didn't help him at all. And he had all sorts of complications."

They're both scanning the paper. Dad actually looks surprised, but Mom's just shaking her head.

She says, "Maybe he didn't have *** good doctor, but Dr. Olsen *** one of *** top cochlear surgeons in *** country. We're fortunate to have *** nearby."

I can't believe I'm beginning to despise my own parents.

I lean forward. Everything's on the line now. We can't keep going back and forth. I'm not going to let them put me under that knife and ruin my ears forever. "I know you called Dr. Brandt, but I'm positive that if she could meet me, she'd change her mind. Please drive me there. For once, don't give up on me."

Mom closes her eyes, like she's tired of this. But I keep going.

"Let's make a list. Together. We can do pros and cons."

"Honey," Dad says, "we can't put this off. If we do, you could be fully deaf sooner than you think. And then we lose time with speech, your schooling, and so many other things. By being proactive now, we can avoid all that."

"What about Bayview?" I'm desperate. "I could keep up with schoolwork there. Maybe it wouldn't be so bad being totally deaf for just a while. Until other, better, options are available." To my own surprise, this doesn't feel like a lie, even though I never seriously considered it before. "Did you know I'm already learning sign language?"

"Your mom and I have talked about it, but—"

"Why is there always a *but*? Why can't we check it out?"

Mom stands. Her hands are flying. "*** want me to send *** to a school four hours away? You're twelve." She paces and yells, "Who will take care *** you when you're sick? Or make sure *** floss your teeth? Or nurse your ear infections? And make sure you eat enough? How can I let someone else care

*** you? And be okay with seeing you so rarely? My God, it's terrifying." She wipes her cheeks.

A tiny part of me wants to hug her. For her to hug me. Because I want her to keep doing all those things for me too. But I also want her to forget the implants. I can't back down on that part. "No, what's terrifying is that surgery. And all the things that could go wrong. And the possibility of it being all for nothing if it doesn't work."

Mom's sobbing into her hands and before I can reach her, Dad does. He cradles her and says to me, "We're done. This is over. Your safety is our number one priority, and we won't risk something else happening to you like the fire alarm incident. The surgery is set, and that's final. Do you understand?"

"I'll never understand." I run to my room and slam the door.

I'm out of choices. It's obvious my parents aren't going to listen to me. Which means I'm going to have to take drastic action.

CHAPTER 20

I messaged Jenika from my iPod a while ago since my parents still have my phone, and I pack as I wait for her to come to my rescue.

Tap, tap, tap.

I slide my window open, and she climbs inside with a bag over her shoulder. "I'm *** sorry. I thought they'd eventually change *** minds."

"Shhh," I put my finger over my lips and whisper. "Thanks for coming."

"I wanted to leave *** soon as I got *** text, but we *** eating dinner."

"It's fine. I had a lot to do."

"*** sure about this?"

The only thing I know for sure is that I'm tired of Mom acting like my ears can be replaced with implants as easily as she replaced our broken dishwasher. They're not the same at all. "I can't sit around anymore and hope something will work out. I have to make something happen for me."

Jenika gives me a hug. "I wish I *** what else to do."

So do I. I'm scared out of my mind, but I've made my decision. "I have to get answers. I'm going to make Dr. Brandt meet with me, and if that doesn't work, I might go all the way to Whitley University in Boston. Someone has to help."

"What?" She wags her finger in my face. "I won't let you leave if *** don't stick to the plan—Orlando *** back. Same day. You can't go all *** way to Boston alone."

I don't say anything.

"Ray!"

I shush her again. "I know, I know."

"Rayne?" She gives me her head-cocked sideways stare.

"I heard you," I whisper.

She unzips the bag she brought. "I packed some stuff *** ***." She pulls out twenty-three dollars in cash, a box of granola bars, four water bottles, and the Helen Keller book . . . again.

"What is it with you and Helen?" I ask.

"Will *** just read about her, at least? She ***

way more than you know."

I toss the book on my bed and stuff a change of clothes into my bag. I'll have to wait for Jenika to leave before I pack even more clothes, or she'll get suspicious about me going to Whitley. But honestly, I will if it's my only choice. Bad people on buses or not, I'd go.

Jenika says, "I love you, *** you need to do what you have to do *** all this, but maybe being deaf isn't *** bad. It wouldn't bother me *** you were. In fact, it might be cool. I'd learn sign *** you and we could tell secrets *** day in school, and no one else would even know what we're saying."

"Except maybe Mr. Faro."

She slaps my arm playfully. "See, you're already ahead. Just think about it." She picks up the book and puts it in my bag. "Helen will be great company *** this trip."

I turn toward my closet, not sure what I'm feeling. I love that Jenika wouldn't care if I were deaf. And maybe I wouldn't mind being deaf, especially if it was temporary till we find another answer. Stem cells or whatever. All I really want right now is time. But staying deaf isn't an option as far as Mom's concerned. She's determined to fix me.

I pull out my stash for the trip, which I hid in my closet earlier this morning: Mom's old TripTik maps (since I can't use GPS without being found), the cleaning kit for my hearing aids, a package of Oreos, my old iPod touch, and cash. I've counted and recounted my money. I really wish I was a better saver, since I only have fifty-six dollars and seventy-five cents in my surfboard bank, but I'm sure it'll be more than enough with the money Jenika's lending me.

"Look at this." I show her my laptop. "The GreenFox bus website says if I buy the ticket online it'll cost me twenty-nine dollars to get to Orlando one way, but if I buy it in person, it will be forty-five dollars. Isn't that so unfair? I can't buy it online without a credit card, and I can't risk using my parents'."

"Yeah, it sucks that *** do that." Jenika folds my sweatshirt and adds it to the bag. "But . . . it might be worth ***. Your parents won't find out right away *** you use it, *** by buying the ticket online, you won't have *** person asking *** why you're traveling alone."

I think on this. "I don't know. I mean, I could be busted either way. But using the credit card at least guarantees that I get *on* the bus. Mom probably won't figure out I'm not at school till at least lunch-time. By then, I'll already be in Orlando."

"Right. And you'll be boarding *** bus home by *** time school's over."

I don't reply.

"Right?" she asks loudly.

"Shhh." I whisper. "Come on, if it costs forty-five in-person dollars just to get to Orlando, I won't be hopping a bus to Boston." Unless I stow away with the luggage or hitchhike there.

"So what's *** plan for getting to the bus?"

I shrug. "I don't have one."

"I swear someone's kidnapped *** real Rayne. This *** not at all like you. You and your detailed life-notebook. Everything perfectly scripted. And now you're running away alone."

"What other option do I have?" My heart skips, and I need a second to breathe. All day I've been keeping as busy as possible, so I don't have to think about that part. "I'm trying hard to be brave here."

"Yeah, sorry. Listen, don't worry. *** be fine."

I will be. I refuse, refuse, refuse to think about the alternatives. If I do, I'll crumble. Chicken out. I'll be stuck here with implants for all eternity.

Jenika says, "You better text me every hour *** give me details."

"I can't bring my phone. My parents would track me."

"What?" She almost yells again but catches herself and says quietly, "You can't go without *** phone. I wouldn't have agreed *** help *** I'd known that."

"I don't have a choice. Unless . . ." I grab the iPod touch. I don't think my parents even remember I have it. "There's this. I can't make phone calls, and it's too risky to text you, but the bus website says the buses have free Wi-Fi."

"Perfect. Create *** new Snap&Share account."

"Yes, then you follow me." I type in the information. When I'm done, I say, "It's under Star Fish. I'll post random pictures to check in. But never of my face. Just in case."

"Star Fish?"

"Stars and the ocean. It's perfect, right?"

"*** smart." She pulls out her phone and adds my fake name.

"Definitely not smart, because I still haven't figured out how to get all the way downtown to the GreenFox terminal."

"What time does *** bus leave?"

"There's one at eight twenty in the morning. I have to at least get dressed for school and pretend I'm going, plus I'll have to convince my mom that I need to ride with you—I'll say we have to make up a science lab or something. So you'll have to be outside tomorrow morning when she drops me off, or she won't believe me. And it means you have to take my bigger bag tonight. I'll keep my backpack with me."

Jenika's quiet for a minute. Finally, she says, "Okay. And I might have an idea for the next part. My dad's marina *** on *** river downtown. You've been there. Let's see how close it is to *** bus station."

She pulls out her phone and types in the two locations on her GPS. "Yes! It's only about four blocks. He usually leaves *** work around seven. *** mom will drop you off at our house, then I *** sneak you into the trunk part *** his truck. He'll never know. Just don't make a sound. Once he's inside his office, *** hop out."

My nerves are shaking my whole insides. It sounds so complicated—not to mention, if Mr. Jackson finds me, I'll be in big trouble before I even get out of town. "I don't know. I need my plan to be foolproof."

"Do you have *** better idea?"

I shake my head. I've run through a bunch of scenarios in my head, but none of them are realistic. At least this one is possible, even if it's risky. "Fine, I'll do it."

"Good." She slides my window open. "You positive I can't come *** you?"

That would make this a whole lot less scary, but it would complicate everything too. "I'll be okay." I will. I have to keep telling myself that. "Thanks so much for your help. I don't know what I'd do without you." It's true. Jenika's the best friend I've ever had. I hope we stay friends for all eternity and more. I hug her tight, and she hugs me back.

"You're going to be *** right, Ray. Even *** Dr. Brandt can't help you, I'm sure she'll tell *** who can."

I swallow hard and nod.

She grabs my bag and hops over the windowsill, yelling, "Take Helen *** you. She's rock-star company."

Ohmygosh. I quickly shut the window and turn up the music in case Mom heard Jenika yell.

I'm going to need a friend to keep my mind off the bazillion and ten things that could happen to me all alone on a bus in a city I hardly know, with people who won't know to talk slowly or clearly for me. I guess Helen will do. I stick the book in my bag and wonder what Helen would have done if her parents had tried to force her to get cochlear implants.

CHAPTER 21

I jump when I hear Mom behind me. Why can't she ever knock? Or did she? Her eyes are red and swollen, and she's holding a tissue. "Troy's here."

I stash my backpack next to my bed, opposite of where she stands, hoping she didn't see how full it is. I hate feeling like everything's so mixed up lately. That seeing Mom makes me feel angry instead of good. That I spent my whole day plotting to run away, instead of having parents who get it—get me. And that knowing Troy's here makes my stomach sink instead of doing somersaults.

When I don't move from my bed, she says, "I told him you'd meet him out front."

"I'll talk to him later." I don't want to see him.

"I'm trying *** be patient *** you, but this is exactly what *** dad and I have been saying. You *** pushing people away. I'm not telling Troy to leave."

"I'm not pushing him away because of my hearing. I've been hanging out with him all this time, haven't I? Do you want me to go out there and tell him I'm fighting with you and Dad about my ears?"

"He's *** good friend. And since you won't talk to us, I'm happy *** you'd at least talk to him. He's waiting."

―――

I take Lucky with me. She's a good distraction, and I won't have to look Troy in the face, because I can't. I can't tell him that I hoped someday something would happen between us, but not anymore. Not after the cups.

He sits on the grass and scratches between Lucky's ears, looking at me when he says, "I *** worried when *** didn't *** my texts and even more when *** mom answered the door. She looks like she's been crying all day."

"They took my phone. I couldn't text."

"Oh. Will *** sit?"

"No, thanks."

"Look, I know *** think I was talking about you when you saw me *** the cups. I mean, I didn't realize at first. You looked really weird, but then I figured out later what *** must've thought."

"You don't have to lie to try to make me feel better."

"I'm not lying! We *** talking about Halloween Horror Nights *** how James is such *** baby about that stuff, so some *** us were just imitating monsters to mess *** him. I swear."

I study his face. His eyes don't leave mine.

"*** have to know by *** I'd never make fun of you."

"Well, you still hurt my feelings, when you realized how awful the implants looked."

"I *** just surprised. But *** that's what you need to hear better, then *** should do it."

"I'll never do that. Never."

"Okay then." He pats the grass. "Will *** at least sit now?"

The grass is cool on my legs, and I purposely keep Lucky between us, because if Troy were to grab my hand again, I might cave in.

He says, "*** not trying to butt ***. I just want to make *** *** okay."

"I wish you wouldn't."

"What?"

"Worry about me. I'm fine."

His fingers brush mine as we both pet Lucky. I yank mine away.

He says, "I'm really trying. I already know *** ears are getting worse. It doesn't bother me."

"Nothing ever does."

"It bothers me that you're upset." He picks a blade of grass.

I hate hurting him. Does he know my ears are getting worse because he can tell, or is he hearing it from his mom, who's probably hearing it from my mom? I wonder, too, if he's being so nice because he feels sorry for me. Maybe that's all this has been. Makes sense since he was so suddenly interested in me in a whole different way.

"And *** pictures. They bothered me *** little too," he says. "Not because *** what they look like, but because I know it bothers you."

"Look." I stand. "I don't need you to feel bad for me."

"What?" He gets to his feet. "I don't."

"Thanks for coming over." I tug on Lucky's leash, so she'll stand. "As you can see, I'm fine. You should go now." It hurts. Way worse than I could have imagined. But I'm leaving tomorrow, and I don't know when I'll be back. Definitely not till I get answers. And I can't even begin to think about figuring out *us* when I haven't figured out *me*.

His face tightens as he studies mine. I have to turn away. I hate how everything's falling apart. I pretty much hate my whole life. But this . . . this is for the best. Mr. Faro's wrong. Sometimes the brakes are necessary.

I walk toward the front door as he spins me around, probably to make sure I hear him loud and clear when he says, "I might only be twelve, but I like you. You've *** my best friend since I was born, but *** way I like you now isn't the same as it was then. I can't explain it. All I know is that when I hear about *** stuff that's happening to you, it makes me mad in *** way I can't put into words. I want to fix everything for you. I can't stand *** world not being a good place for you. And it freaks me out a little too, because I'm not even sure where it's coming from. But I don't care if you can't hear. I don't care if you get implants. I don't care if you wait *** stem cells. I'm pretty sure none of those things are going to make me stop liking you. None *** them will make me want to stop fixing the world for you."

I had no idea he knew all the details, and I don't

know if I should be embarrassed or grateful. I believe him. Every word. He doesn't feel sorry for me after all. He doesn't see me as broken. He doesn't want to fix me. He wants to fix the rest of the world *for* me.

I look skyward and blink over and over. As much as I love that he doesn't care one bit that I can't hear, I do. Not just Mom and Dad. Me. Maybe that's been my problem all along.

"And you know what, Star Girl?" He leans in and kisses my cheek. "I'd even give Arcturus my eyeball for you."

He doesn't wait for me to answer before he takes off, and I'm glad for that, because how could I possibly respond? How do you tell someone you're so glad they see you as the person you want to be, only you don't see yourself that way anymore? And the truth is, you probably never will again.

I don't sleep at all. Instead, I worry about missing my bus. Or the bus people not letting me get on.

Confidence. That's all it will take. And concentration. Watch every person's lips. Pay extra attention. But don't stand out.

I don't know if I can do this.

I've never been great at praying, but I'm desperate, so I give it another try. *Hey, I hope you remember me. I'm sorry it's been so long, but um, I'm about to run away. You probably already know that, but the thing is, I don't want to. Is there a way you can make Mom and Dad listen to me? I'm afraid to get on that bus, so if you could give me a sign that I don't need to, that would be great. Like maybe in the morning, Mom and Dad will say that we can wait awhile to figure things out. Thanks. I'll be looking for it. Amen from me.*

A sign. Stay? Go?

The clock says 3:46 a.m. Lucky's probably snoring—I can see her head jerking back and forth, but I can't be sure without my aids in. I pet her warm belly and then reach for my laptop. I don't want to get on that bus. Maybe the implants won't be so bad. Maybe Mom's right.

I should stay. It's safe here.

I pull Lucky onto my lap and then check the cochlear implant board again, hoping to talk one-on-one with someone who's happily implanted, but instead I read a note from Jillian, who private-messaged me and whose head is still bleeding four weeks after surgery and whose implants can't be activated because the swelling is ginormous. There are others too. Each one just as awful. I must be gasping out loud because Lucky jolts awake and stares at me.

No, no, no. I can't do it. I have to leave.

CHAPTER 22

My stomach's a mess. If Mom sees me like this, she'll make me stay home. Worse, she'll stay home with me. Then I'll never escape.

She comes in to wake me—which isn't necessary since I haven't slept even thirty seconds all night—and looks puzzled when she sees I'm already dressed. "*** up early."

"Yeah," I say. "Jenika and I have to finish our lab report on Newton's Law since I . . . you know . . . ran out that day."

Mom's quiet. Does she know something's up? Did she hear me sneak into the kitchen and go through her purse for the credit card in the middle of the night?

I wipe my hand across my forehead. It's suddenly hot in my room.

She says, "*** dad and I *** hoping to have breakfast *** you."

This must be my sign. "You're changing your mind about the implants?"

"Honey, it's not that simple."

"Yes, it is. You just cancel the surgery. We talk to more doctors."

She rubs her temples. "Someday, when you're *** mom, you'll understand."

"Nope, I don't need to hear your thoughts over breakfast then. I can't be late, or Jenika and I will both get zeros."

"Fine, *** only because it would be unfair to her. Tonight, we *** talking. Like it or not. We *** to come together. For ***, I'll drive *** over. I won't have *** skipping school again."

Come together? I almost laugh out loud, but instead, I grab my backpack, grateful that I was smart enough to give Jenika my bag last night. I head out the door, turning back only long enough to do two things: place the message board notes that I printed out on my bed, hoping my parents will finally read the horror stories after I'm gone, and give Lucky a big squeeze and a kiss on the snout. I hope she won't be mad if I'm gone too long. But there's no time to worry about that. I have a bus to catch.

The white curtain falls away from Jenika's living room window and within two seconds, she's skidding out the front door. She waves to my mom, and when Mom's gone, Jenika says, "What took you so long?"

"Am I late?"

"No, but . . ." She sighs. "Just . . . let's do this fast. Daddy's already dressed and on his second cup of coffee. Which means he's leaving any second."

Each time I'm about to chicken out—like right now—I think of the awful stories from the message boards. So without hesitation, I climb into the trunk of Mr. Jackson's SUV because anything is better than implants.

"Hey." Jenika reaches out her hand. "I didn't think I'd be *** nervous, but uh, make sure *** check in. A lot! Okay?"

I reach out my hand to squeeze hers. "I will. I promise." I dig in my pocket and hand her an index card with my bus information. "In case someone steals me."

"Not funny."

"I'm not trying to be." But I laugh anyway.

Because what else can I do besides freak out? And I refuse to do that. For both our sakes. "I'm going to be fine. Like you said last night. I've planned out everything I'm going to say to Dr. Brandt." I've even come up with a cover story so that she won't immediately realize I'm a runaway from halfway across the state. Once she sees how determined I am and agrees to give me a spot in the study, *then* I'll tell her who I really am and where I'm really from.

Jenika says, "Remember, confidence is *** key. No one will mess *** you if you act sure *** yourself."

I nod, hoping I can pull that off.

She looks toward the house, then at me. "I better go, or you'll never even make it out of the neighborhood."

I swallow the lump in my throat. "Right. Listen, Jenika. You're my best friend in the whole world. Sometimes I'm not sure how I got so lucky. I'm going to be fine, and I'll check in constantly. Don't worry. Okay?"

"I'll try. But *** there's any trouble, you better borrow someone's *** phone and call me immediately. Promise?"

"I promise."

"Okay. Good luck. Knock Dr. Brandt out *** her mind with your charm."

"I plan to."

She hesitates a second longer and finally closes the hatch. She places her palm on the window, but I don't reach to match her. I don't want her to see my hand shaking. Instead, I look away, hoping that Mr. Jackson's done with his coffee and that he doesn't have to put anything in the trunk.

CHAPTER 23

Jenika's a genius. The plan works perfectly, probably because Mr. Jackson is on a phone call the entire way downtown and never once suspects I'm all the way in the back. After he gets out, I wait a few minutes before popping my head up. The coast is clear, so I click the trunk's inside release button and climb out. Before my foot even hits the pavement, the alarm blares, sending my hearing aids screeching.

Ohmygosh! I take off running as fast as I can. Straight ahead. Not even sure which direction I'm going. As I round a brick building, I drop my bags, try to catch my breath, and then peek back around the corner. Mr. Jackson's inspecting his car—trunk wide open. I hide when he glances around, obviously looking for a suspect, and starts walking my way. Even though I'm already out of breath, I didn't make it this far to be caught now, so I grab my bags and take off.

A few blocks away, I locate street names and then look at my hand-drawn map. But nothing matches up. I must have run in the wrong direction, and I don't have time to figure this out alone or I might miss the bus. I scan the faces of people walking by, hoping to pick a nice one. There's a lady in a red business suit carrying a briefcase. She's checking texts or something on her phone.

"Excuse me," I say. "Can you tell me where the GreenFox bus station is?"

Her phone rings, and she answers. "Hello, hang *** *** second, ***." To me she says, "***, *** idea." She walks into an office building.

I scan more faces and decide on a man in a suit drinking coffee as he leans against the same office building. "Excuse me, can you tell me where Locust and Third Street meet, please?"

"Locust?" He shakes his head. "Sorry. I *** Third *** that way." He points toward my left.

I have no clue how far I have to go, and panic sets in. I'm really going to miss the bus now. What if it's ten blocks from here? What if it's thirty? What if Mom knows I'm gone and is already looking for me? I yell as loud as I can, "Does anyone know where the GreenFox bus station is on Third and Locust Streets?"

I get a lot of stares, but no one offers an answer. Just as I think I might lose it, a man sitting on a ripped-up cardboard box near an alley says, "*** *** way. Go *** blocks *** ***, *** *** right, and Locust *** *** *** ** blocks."

I have to go closer if I want to hear him, and even though I'm a little scared, I feel like this guy's okay. So I lean in. "I'm sorry. I can't hear well. What did you say?"

He repeats, "Go three blocks to Third, hang a right, and Locust is up two more blocks."

I repeat it, to make sure I got it right, and he nods. "Thank you, thank you!" I say. I reach in my backpack and pull out a granola bar.

He takes it and leans over, almost like he's bowing. "Bless you."

It sure doesn't feel like I'm blessed. "You're welcome." I start to move away but turn back. "What's your name?"

"Steven."

"Thanks, Steven."

I run, as fast as I can, to catch my bus.

I make it to Locust and Third in ten minutes, but this can't be the right spot. All I see is a tiny building, like smaller than a 7-11. There are no buses, no bus stalls for them to pull into like at Disney, and no people. I double-check the address in my notebook. It says this is it. The building's surrounded by car shops, all packed with people. I don't want to stand here too long and stick out, so I inch behind a tree, wondering what to do. From there, I spot a small yellow sign with a picture of a green fox on it bolted to the side of the building. This must be the right place after all.

Confidence. Like Jenika said. I can do this.

I straighten my shoulders and stride into the GreenFox station. I pause only long enough to look around once before escaping to the bathroom. Inside, I lean against the cold, yellow-tiled wall and remind myself to breathe. It's not how I pictured it, but it's not horrible either. I go over the scene in my head. I counted maybe fifteen people total. The girl selling tickets looks about the same age as the kids at Dad's school and didn't seem to be super enthused about her job, so hopefully she won't even notice I'm alone. I'll be fine. This will work.

Confidence, I repeat to myself. I smile in the blurry, scratched-up mirror, and head to the waiting room.

Without much thought, I take the closest empty seat and end up next to a girl who looks like she's around Colby's age. Maybe she's even going back to school or something. She's dressed in all black with an unbuttoned baggy denim shirt over top and white sandals. She sees me staring and gives me a *what-are-you-looking-at* face.

I point. "I was just admiring your headphones." They're hot pink and chunky, with the earmuff parts spiking out—almost like cochlear implants but bigger. And removable.

She lifts one side away from her ear. "What?"

"Sorry," I say. "I was just admiring your headphones. They're pretty awesome."

"Thanks." She lets the earmuff fall back to her head, her long blond hair now a little bit tangled in it. But I don't dare tell her.

She raises it again. "What *** it?"

"Nothing. Um, do you live here? Are you headed on a trip or something?"

"I don't live anywhere." She drops the earmuff again and smacks her gum while she scrolls through the playlist on her phone.

How does someone not live anywhere? I study her face, but when she sees I'm still staring, I physically turn myself away so I won't do it again. For some reason, though, I feel a little safer next to her.

I snap a photo of my fingers throwing the peace sign with the ticket counter in the background. I caption it *Waiting for a fox* and post it. I'm sure Jenika is already hitting the love button.

Outside the double glass doors to my left, a bus pulls in. My heart's beating so fast, I push on my chest to try to get it to calm down.

The girl behind the counter calls out. "*** *** *** *** *** arri***. *** *** *** *** *** *** ***."

There's no getting my heart to slow now. This is exactly what I was afraid of. I look around. There's no board listing bus numbers or times. Some people stand. The girl next to me doesn't. How do I know if I should? I could ask the girl behind the counter. But what if she asks why I'm alone?

I don't know what to do.

But I have to do something.

I stand and walk toward the wall, hoping to see something, anything, that will tell me if this is my bus or not.

It pulls around the building and stops outside the glass doors to my right. A second bus pulls in next to it. The girl behind the counter yells again, but I can't understand a word.

The two drivers, both older men, come inside.

One of them says, "*** *** *** *** two lines." He points to the rope divider.

I can't.

I just can't.

Everything's moving so slowly, like I'm stuck in a movie, but it's going on without me. My feet are glued, but I have to move. Now. Pick a bus, hope it's the right one. I seriously hate my ears.

Someone taps my shoulder from behind, and I yelp out loud. Every single face turns toward me.

Confidence, confidence, confidence, I scream inside my head, but my body can't pull itself together.

The girl with the pink headphones says, "I didn't mean to scare ***. *** seriously paler *** *** ghost."

I don't answer.

"*** *** okay?" she asks.

I nod, short and fast, and turn away from her to face the guys checking tickets. Just pick one.

"*** seriously look lost. Are *** alone?"

"No. No, uh, my mom, she's coming."

"Right." She rolls her eyes. "Look, I get it. I've been *** *** shoes. Why don't *** tell me where *** going?"

"To see a doctor."

She laughs. "***, what city? What does ***
ticket say?"

I pull it out of my backpack and show her.

She hands it back to me. "*** in luck. I'm *** the
same bus—express to Orlando."

"Cool!" I bite my lip, hoping to play off my relief
and keep her from thinking I'm a total weirdo. "So,
did you, by chance, hear which line we're supposed
to get in?"

"That one."

I smile. "Thanks." I move toward the line on the
right, Pink Headphone Girl behind me. But when I
look ahead to the man taking the tickets and checking IDs, my knees give out. I grab onto the metal
pole that separates the two lines, and it crashes to the
floor, tightening the rope attached to it, which yanks
the next pole to the ground too. The only thing that
keeps me from falling is Pink Headphone Girl behind
me, who grabs me by my armpit and heaves me up.

Not letting go of me, she pulls me out of line and
over to the wall. "*** pretty sure I get what's going
*** here, but if *** don't stop causing scenes, they'll
never let *** ***."

My chest is tight. So tight. I came all this way,
and it's over already. I don't have an ID. I never in

a million years thought they'd ask for one, but I should've known they would. All of this, for nothing. Mom and Dad will lock me up for the rest of my life, and I didn't even get a chance to meet Dr. Brandt first.

I sink to the floor.

"Dramatic, much?" the girl asks.

"Please, leave me alone."

She smacks her gum loudly while looking me over. "I should. Yeah, I should walk ***. But what is *** problem? *** obviously have *** reason to get *** *** bus."

"I do, but I don't have an ID."

"Oh, come ***. They hardly even check."

"But I don't have *anything*. Not even a school ID."

She sighs. "It's not that big *** deal. I'll say *** with me."

"You'd do that? You think it will work?"

She blows a bubble and says, "It's a bus station. Really."

"Okay." I get to my feet, feeling a whole lot better than sixty seconds ago. "Thank you."

"But it *** *** you."

I heard a *c*, but what else? "I'm sorry, what?"

"Ten bucks." She holds out her hand. "I gotta eat, *** know."

I wait for her to laugh and say gotcha or something.

"Or *** can hang here at *** station. *** choice."

The line's empty now. If we don't move, we'll both miss the bus. "Fine." I dig in my backpack for a ten-dollar bill and hand it to her.

She stuffs it in her pocket and leads me toward the door. The man checks both her ticket and her ID. Pink Headphone Girl says, "*** is my cousin. *** meeting *** dad in Orlando to go to Disney."

I give him my ticket, and he doesn't even ask for identification. He doesn't comment on Disney either. He just hands my ticket back and waves us onto the bus. I can't believe it worked. I smile but quickly try to hide it—playing it cool.

On the bus, I take a window seat, making room for Pink Headphone Girl next to me, but she passes right by and sits in the row behind. It's fine. I don't want to get stuck paying her for anything else anyway. And I'm glad I don't have to strain to hear a conversation for the next few hours, especially since I didn't sleep at all last night, and I'm already tired. This is better. This is great. I can't believe I'm doing this on my own, and that in a few hours, I'll be meeting with Dr. Brandt. Finally.

But I also can't help wondering what Pink Headphone Girl's story is. This is definitely not her first bus trip. Does she spend her whole life running? She may have perfect ears, but I'm guessing she doesn't have a perfect life. I think about Jenika, Troy, Colby, and even Mom and Dad. I look at the girl again. Suddenly, I don't feel jealous of her hearing. I kinda just feel sorry for her.

CHAPTER 24

The bus seems brand new. Its leather seats are practically shining, and the bathroom is spotless. Now that we're actually on the road, I don't know what I was ever afraid of. It takes me a few tries to connect to the Wi-Fi, but once that's done, I take another photo, this time aimed out the window, to show I'm on my way. When I go to post it, I see Jenika's liked my first one, and there's a shiny blinking star near the top corner—six new follow requests from people I don't know and twelve from kids at my school who don't even follow my real account.

For a second this bothers me. Okay, more than a second, but there's no way any of them know it's me, and I like that I can literally be anyone right now. *Click.* Added! I plug the iPod touch into the charging outlet between the two seats in front of me, so excited for the first time in forever.

That is, until I notice the guy in the seat across the aisle, dressed all nice and with perfectly placed hair. He's staring at me and smiling. I turn my whole body to face the window and hope he'll fall asleep or something. But I can see in the window reflection that he's watching me.

We stop at a tiny bus station in the middle of nowhere. Seriously, there's nothing around and the building is even smaller than the one we were in before. The guy next to me is still stare-smiling, so I grab my bags and get off the bus, hoping to use the bathroom or stretch or something, but I'm double creeped out when the man follows me down the steps.

I do a quick stretch, turn around, and get right back on. This time, I move to the row behind Pink Headphone Girl, ducking low into the seat and hoping the guy won't notice me when he gets back on. If he gets back on.

Sure enough, he gets back on.

Peeking between two seats, I see he's looking around and walking past his last spot.

"*** *** *** leave *** alone." The girl has her headphones around her neck and what seems like a *don't-mess-with-me* look on her face, though I can only see the side of it.

The guy doesn't say a word. He just walks to his original spot toward the front. I want to thank the girl, but she's already listening to her music again, head bobbing.

My whole body's shaking. What would have happened if she hadn't noticed him? I don't even want to think about it. I grab my sweatshirt from my bag, put it on, and pull the hood over my head, hoping I can stay invisible for the rest of the trip.

———

R-Jarrow's been keeping me company. I'm trying hard to memorize the sound of her voice, in case I eventually never hear her again. I can hardly believe it when we pull into the GreenFox station in Orlando. It's huge.

As we get up, the girl with the pink headphones takes them off. "*** luck *** *** doctor." She follows me down the steps and then heads toward another bus.

"I thought you said you were going to Orlando?"

"Yeah, but only *** a connection to Tampa."

"Tampa?" Part of me wishes I could go with her, to see Colby. "Do you have family there?"

"Nope."

On the platform, there must be a hundred or more people. "Well, thanks again. For your help and all." Maybe I shouldn't say this since I paid for her help, but she did more than a lot of people might've done. "What's your name anyway?"

When I don't hear her answer, I assume it's because I'm not facing her, but when I turn around, she's gone. I spot her in line a few slots over. The front of that bus says 3611. I really am clueless when I don't focus. This whole time the bus number was on the front, and I didn't even know. I guess if I had known, I might have never met that girl, and I definitely wouldn't have gotten on the bus without her claiming me. She turns and waves before boarding, and I mouth, *Thank you.* She tosses her chin in the air, as if to say *No problem*, and a moment later she disappears—making it seem so easy.

The inside of the Orlando station looks a lot like an airplane terminal, with boards showing arrivals and departures. There's a small food court, a ginormous waiting area, six ticket takers, and a whole lot of people who look like they haven't had a shower in forever asking for money. Thankfully, there's no sign of the guy from the bus. And thankfully, there are lockers—five bucks for the whole day. No need to carry my just-in-case-I-go-all-the-way-to-Boston bag full of clothes. I stash the duffel bag in locker 315, double-check the latch, and hope my stuff will be safe while I'm gone.

I pull my backpack closer and dart out the front door.

My TripTik map of Orlando says it's twenty-three blocks to Dr. Brandt's office. Heck, I've walked triple that amount at Disney World. This will be no problem.

But unlike at Disney, there aren't a lot of people walking here, and the road I'm following, Highway 50, is surrounded by buildings that look older than my parents added together. After one block, I'm dripping sweat. By the time I reach block eighteen, my hair's plastered to my head. My shirt's plastered to my body. There's no way I can see Dr. Brandt like this, so I make a detour across the street into a McDonald's until I can dry off. After a $4.50 happy meal, my face can't stop smiling. I'm so close now.

As soon as I cross under a highway, the scenery changes. The medical building where Dr. Brandt's office is located is raised up, with an open parking lot under it. It's surrounded by huge oak trees and a path that leads around a sparkly lake with a sign that says *Lake Adair*. I've never seen trees this pretty back home. I snap a photo, and once I'm in the lobby and find a free Wi-Fi spot, I post it to my account.

#dayoff #wishyouwereme

The papers I printed show a photo of Dr. Brandt, who looks like she's probably the same age as Mom. Her dark skin kinda glows, and she looks super athletic too, like maybe she'd go surfing with me once she fixes my ears. Will the stem cells fix my balance too? I hope so. Everything feels so exciting now. I find the suite number and ride the elevator to the third floor.

Outside the door, there's a clear box with a bunch of brochures. I look for one about the study she's doing, but I only find general information about spine care, strokes, brain injuries, and hearing loss. There's also a brochure for the Bayview School for the Deaf and Blind. Weird! Why would she want people to know about that school when she can fix their ears? They wouldn't need Bayview. I take one, figuring I'll ask her about it.

My hands slide along the nameplate next to the door. *Dr. Brandt, Neurosurgery.* She must be really, really smart. And I have to be totally convincing. I rehearse the lines in my head one last time and open the door to the waiting room.

There's not a single person here. It's almost one o'clock, so maybe everyone's at lunch, or maybe she has all her trial people inside already. Maybe they spend the whole day together doing tests and stuff.

I knock on the glass window.

A woman slides it open. "*** *** I help ***?"

"Hi." Big smile. "I'm here to see Dr. Brandt about her clinical trial. I have sudden sensorineural hearing loss and would like to discuss it with her."

She stands and peeks through the window, around the waiting room. "Where *** your parents?"

"They couldn't make it today. They sent me to get the information, and I'm supposed to bring it to them."

"I see. *** *** *** second, please." She closes the window.

Jenika's right. This confidence thing works.

A few seconds later, the lady appears again. "I'm

sorry, I *** *** *** manager, *** without a parent, I can't *** *** *** information."

I lean in, with my right ear straining to hear her. She repeats, "Sorry. I said, I can't give you any information without a parent here."

"Oh, that's okay. I don't really need the information. I can just speak with Dr. Brandt."

Her smile goes flat. "If you'd like to *** *** appointment, please *** *** parent call ***." She emphasizes. "We're not allowed *** speak to minors."

I hate that word. Like so much. My face must show how mad I am because the lady backs away and reaches for the phone.

She says, "Do *** need *** to pick *** up? *** *** look well."

I don't answer.

"Shouldn't *** be in school? Are ***—"

I don't wait for her to finish. I bolt out before she can connect all the dots.

I run. All the way to the lake, and when I get there, I crash onto a wooden bench and try to pull myself together. So far, I've successfully run away, outsmarted a bus driver, walked twenty-two blocks, and found Dr. Brandt's office. I cannot turn back now. I know Dr. Brandt is in that building. She has to be. I walk back toward it and wander through the parking lot underneath. There's a row of cars parked in front of signs that read *Physician Parking Only.* I decide to wait. For as long as I need to. She has to come out sometime.

CHAPTER 25

Three hours and ten Oreos later, I'm sleepy as I lie on the cool half wall that outlines the parking garage. I've watched parents push kids in strollers around the lake, flipped through the Bayview school brochure again, and learned a lot about Helen Keller.

It turns out she only threw tantrums because she was frustrated that she couldn't communicate. She was born hearing and seeing but lost both senses when she got sick as a little kid, so I get it. Helen felt totally cut off from the world till her private teacher, Ms. Sullivan, took her to a water pump one day and ran her hand under it. Then Ms. Sullivan spelled *w-a-t-e-r* with her finger on Helen's hand. I guess that's all she needed for things to click. The book says Helen describes it as the moment her soul woke up. Once she understood finger spelling, she started learning things superfast and everything changed.

She eventually became a humanitarian, traveling the world and speaking up for what she believed in. She didn't care what anyone thought.

What gets me, though, is that she came to really appreciate the unique way she experienced the world. Not better than anyone else. Not worse. Just different.

I stare out at the lake and try to take the whole thing in. I try to imagine living my life as if my hearing loss isn't the only important thing about me. Is it possible? All the options I've considered—hearing aids, implants, or being deaf—still leave me with the same questions. Will my hearing loss ever stop being all my family—and even I—talk and think about? Will it ever just be part of who I am?

Or maybe stem cells will be my breakthrough like finger spelling was for Helen.

I'm about to pop another Oreo in my mouth when I spot Dr. Brandt coming out of the elevator in the garage. I run over to her. "Dr. Brandt."

Her eyes are wide and questioning.

As much as my head screams at me to stay calm, my mouth doesn't cooperate. Everything rushes out—the truth mixed in with the cover story I created. "I live here in Orlando, just over there." I point toward the houses past the lake. "My audiologist says I'm losing my hearing, and it's getting worse. My parents and I did some research and found out about your trial, and we're so happy because my mom saved my umbilical cord when I was born. My parents are going to call you, but I couldn't wait for another second to see you. To see if you'd make an exception and let me in your study, even though you may think I'm too old. I'm begging you—beg, beg, begging you—to let me in."

She sticks her hand out. "Slow down." She shakes her head, like she's thinking. "Can you hear me?"

I nod.

"Okay, well, it's good you're doing *** research now, but if *** can still hear, I imagine you have a lot *** time before you have to make any major decisions."

Was Mom lying to me about what Dr. Brandt told her? "I keep telling my parents that."

She sets her briefcase on the ground. "Science *** amazing. There *** promising things coming, but my trial started six months ago, even if I disregarded *** age—which I can't do—*** too much you've missed."

"Six months is not a big deal. I can move here

and catch up. I'll work hard until I'm where everyone else is."

"Move here? Didn't you say *** live here?"

"Oh, yeah. I meant, move into your office. You
know, if your patients have to stay all the time."

Her face cocks sideways and she stares off behind
me for a few seconds, like she's thinking. "You need
to understand *** it works. These trials take years
*** get approved. Even *** I wanted to bend ***
rules, I can't."

"Well, what about other studies? Do you know
one I can get in?"

She shakes her head. "No, but just because
you're not in them doesn't mean *** results won't
help ***."

"They won't help if I already have the implants!"

"What did *** say?" She leans in.

"You don't understand. My parents are willing
to consider a trial like this, but they said if it doesn't
work out, they'll make me get cochlear implants.
Isn't there anything you can do?"

Her shoulders drop. "This is sounding familiar.
*** live over there?" She tilts her head again. "What
did *** say your name is?"

I don't answer.

"*** know." She points at me. "I had a lady call me recently about this same thing, but she lived—"

No. I can't let this get messed up. "I promise, if you just give me a chance, you'll see I'm a good person for your study. I'll do anything."

She reaches for my shoulder. "Come to my office *** me." She's dialing a number.

Please let it be the person who can give her permission to change the study. She's not sending me away, so that has to be a good sign, right? I practically skip to the elevator with her.

"Sarah, hi. Can *** get me *** *** emergency police number? *** *** my way back up."

What? No! Did I hear that right? This can't be happening.

The elevator doors open, and Dr. Brandt steps inside, but I take off. Tears fall with every step that leads me farther away from what was my last hope. My last chance.

CHAPTER 26

The long walk back to the bus station hasn't helped me calm down or clear my head. I can't go home. I could try to get to Boston, but if that doesn't work out either, then what? It's not like I can ride the bus forever, like Pink Headphone Girl. Or can I? Maybe she's trying to find answers too. I wonder what her questions are. I wonder if either of us will ever find what we need.

My stomach's growling, so I grab my stuff from the locker and head to the cafeteria in the bus station, where I scan the menu for the cheapest food option. I settle on a burger and fries for five dollars plus a cup of water.

It all tastes like sadness.

I dig through my backpack for the iPod, but instead I end up pulling out the brochure for Bayview. There's a small map in the corner of the pamphlet, which shows that the school is right on the Gulf of Mexico in St. Petersburg. Near Tampa. The kid from the ChannelThis video did like a mini-tour, and honestly, the campus looked awesome: beautiful brick buildings, huge trees, a river, even a beach. But that's not what got me most. It was all the things he said he was involved in, like at any other high school, but I wonder how the students can do all those things if they can't hear. Maybe it helps that all the kids have similar needs. What does it even feel like to not worry about hearing or not hearing because everyone's in the same situation?

The questions swirl in my head. If Dr. James recommended it and Dr. Brandt had the brochure outside her office door, maybe they're signs that I should at least check out this school. It's a lot closer than Whitley University.

———

The girl behind the counter is picking orange polish off her super long nail.

"I need a ticket to St. Petersburg, please."

"*** *** *** *** tonight?" She sounds almost like she's talking in a whole other language. I can hardly understand her, not to mention that the GreenFox bus station is packed, so it's extra noisy.

"I'm sorry. I didn't understand you. I need it for tonight, if that's what you asked."

"*** *** two. Both *** *** Gainesville ***. One *** *** to Jacksonville. *** other *** Tampa." She flicks her eyes to me, waiting for my answer.

I don't know what it is about her, but I can't read her lips at all. My heart is shaking my insides. "No, one ticket. I don't care where I go first. I just need it to end in St. Petersburg. Can you give me that one?"

"*** be thirty-*** dollars." She holds out her palm.

I can't mess this up. "And you're sure it's to St. Petersburg?"

Major eye roll.

"Sorry. Okay. Thank you." I hand her forty dollars in cash because I'm not sure the exact amount she said, but I know it was in the thirties. She gives me three back, along with the ticket. I'm glad to be done with her, but my stomach feels a little sick when I register that I only have $18.25 left. And no intention of going home soon. I'll have to be better about saving.

On the platform outside, I look at the monitor above and find the lane that says 4812. There's already a line of people, even though the bus doesn't leave till nine thirty—another twenty minutes. My body's achy, and I'm so tired. My hope is fading, but it's not gone.

When the bus finally comes, I hang back. The driver looks barely old enough to have a license, and he's joking with the people in line while he checks their IDs. I slide in behind a guy and a girl who have been kissing for the last ten minutes and pray I can pull this off. The kissing couple both have big suitcases, and as soon as the driver turns around and rolls them toward the underside compartment near the middle of the bus, I dart up the steps as fast as possible. Unnoticed! I can't believe it worked.

This bus isn't new like the one from this morning. Instead, the smell of urine and stale food hits me as soon as I reach the top step. That, mixed with the gross hamburger I ate, makes me want to hurl. I decide to sit in the back, near the bathroom, just in case. Not that there are many open seats to pick from anyway. The stink is even worse here, though. I go for the closest open seat and hope my sweatshirt pulled over my face will cover the smell.

A guy with a long ponytail looks at the empty seat next to me. Please, no! His bright-striped shirt looks like something Ernie from *Sesame Street* would wear. It's tucked into his underwear, which is sticking out above his baggy jeans. He slumps next to me and shoves his camo bag under the seat.

"*** *** I sit here?" he mumbles, after he already is.

"I guess." I turn toward the window, hoping it's not rude, but also hoping to avoid talking. I plug my charger into the outlet, but before I connect it, I check the Snap&Share app. One hundred and twenty-six new follow requests. I can't believe it. I'm more popular than the real me, which definitely bothers me. On the bright side, though, I can be anyone I want with this, like a cool girl who travels the state and doesn't have a hearing problem.

I spot Jenika's comment on my last post. *Where are you? Everyone's freaking.*

That was at eight. And a few minutes ago she posted: *Rayne, you promised.*

Wow, so everyone knows it's me. So much for being anonymous.

Jenika's probably told my parents our whole plan. My plan.

None of this is her fault. But I've given Mom and Dad every chance to change their minds. I'll keep running, like Pink Headphone Girl, until they agree to cancel the operation. Even if I do have to go to Whitley alone. Even if I have to steal money to get there.

I comment on my own photo, tagging Jenika. *Did they change their minds?*

I refresh instantly, hoping for a quick reply. You know, since everyone's supposedly out of their mind with worry. But there's nothing.

The old me was not patient. But the old me would never have taken a trip like this either. No more checking social media. I'm going to do what I have to do and that's it. I delete the Snap&Share app and shove the iPod in my pocket.

Once we're almost to the highway, the bus driver clicks on the intercom and says, "Welcome *** GreenFox *** *** ***. *** *** no smoking *** *** alcohol. *** *** trash bins *** *** back. *** *** *** ***. *** *** *** final *** Jacksonville *** *** two a.m."

I bolt up in my seat, tapping the guy next to me. "Did he say Jacksonville?"

"Yeah."

"Do we have to go through St. Petersburg to get to Jacksonville?" Geography has never been my best subject, but I know Tampa and Jacksonville are on opposite sides of the state.

"I dunno. I just get *** *** bus *** ride." He's nodding like he's all chill with life, but my insides are about to explode.

"Excuse me," I practically yell, jumping over his legs. For once, I'm going to have to ask for more help.

There's a clear piece of plastic, almost like a door, separating me from the driver. I shout over it to make sure he hears me. "I'm sorry, but is this the bus to St. Petersburg?"

He doesn't turn to face me, so I can't hear anything he's saying.

Dang it. I try to whisper-talk. "I'm sorry. I can't hear well. Can you repeat that?"

He cups his ear, like he can't hear me either.

This stinks. Like so bad. I'm going to have to shout, and everyone will hear, but what choice do I have? "I have hearing loss, so I don't know what you're saying, but I *really* need to be on the bus to St. Petersburg, and I think you said Jacksonville."

"If you're going to St. Pete, you're on the wrong

bus." He laughs, and that I hear clearly. "*** *** not show me *** ticket? I would have told ***."

"Can you please turn the bus around? We're not that far."

This time he does look at me . . . like I'm totally nuts.

"Well, can you pull over and let me out here? Maybe I can take a cab back to the station?"

"Girl, *** stuck *** *** least *** first stop, *** *** Gainesville."

"No! I have to get off now." I rattle the plastic between us.

"*** only *** *** getting off *** *** I call *** cops. Now cut *** out."

I will not cry. I won't. Every single person on the bus stares at me as I walk to my seat. I suck in a deep breath and almost choke on the stink. I shake my head and close my eyes. I can do this. It's just a small detour.

The guy next to me is snoring, and I hope I won't wake him, but I switch the light on and take out my map of Florida. I have no clue why the bus from Orlando to Jacksonville would go through Gainesville, but at least this weird route saves me from ending up clear on the other side of the state.

Suddenly, my left hearing aid beeps into my ear. I dig through my backpack and pull out an empty battery package.

It hits me: I didn't put hearing aid batteries on my packing list. How could I have forgotten them? I can barely do anything without my aids.

Signs—these must all be signs that I'm not supposed to be here. But I'm not supposed to be home either. Or in Orlando. Or on this bus. Clearly, I'm not supposed to be anywhere.

———

The bus rolls into the Gainesville station around midnight. It's completely deserted, and I'm the only one who gets off. I ask my driver, "Will there be any other buses coming tonight?"

He motions for me to look at him, and he says, "There is one to Tampa. It should be here any minute."

I'm grateful to understand him since I'm working with just one ear now. "Okay, thanks."

As he's driving away, the new bus rounds the corner ahead.

I take the iPod from my pocket to check the time, and like my hearing aid battery, it's dead. As I unzip my backpack, I realize I never unplugged my charger from the port on the bus.

Oh no. No, no, no.

I run after the first bus screaming, "Wait!" My arms wave wildly as I keep chasing that green fox, whose face I'd swear is laughing at me as it gets farther and farther away.

The lights from bus #6489 spotlight my desperation as it pulls in. I shield my eyes and turn away, looking for a ticket counter. But there's nothing here except a little machine with a big sign saying *Tickets: Credit only. No cash.* And I don't have ID to show the driver anyway.

No. Just no. I can't do this anymore. The whole wide world is sending me messages, and I haven't been listening.

I'm hungry.

I haven't slept in two days.

I'm done.

I fall onto a bench and wish that I could just go home.

A lady bus driver with silver hair shuffles over to me. "*** *** okay?"

I feel . . . heavy. And tired. Out of choices. Out of hope. I explain my mix-up with the last bus and confess that I don't have a credit card to buy a new ticket from the machine. "Will you take cash? Or this ticket, since I just got on the wrong bus?"

"*** *** *** *** *** *** *** *** Orlando."

I shake my head. I can't hear her. I can't even read her lips. "I'm sorry. So sorry." I burst into sobs right there at the bus station, in the middle of the night, because as much as I've been lying to myself, I can't anymore. "I can't hear," I cry. "I can't hear a single thing." I show her my hearing aids, something I've never done to anyone other than Jenika. "And I'm a liar!"

This trip is harder than I ever thought it would be. School is hard. Surfing is hard. Music is practically gone. I barely have any friends left, and even though I'm class president, I can't do my job. The truth of how much my life has changed hurts my whole insides, but I can't pretend anymore. Lying is exhausting.

"My parents are right. I do need implants." My body's shaking with the reality of it all. The whole world has become my Box of Shame, and it seems like the only way to tear down its walls is to get the implants.

The bus driver's sitting next to me, pulling me into her soft, pillowy body. Letting me have my cry.

When I'm done, I look up, and she says, "What're *** going to St. Pete ***?"

"To see a school for kids like me."

"Well then, *** best hop on my bus," she says. "*** don't give up on dreams on my watch. *** hear me?"

I can't tell if she meant that as in, do I literally hear her, or as in like, do I get what she's saying—but either way, I'm glad she's not leaving me stranded here.

"*** *** got someone pickin' you up *** Tampa?"

I start to feel a little better. Like maybe I shouldn't give up yet. So I lie again. Because if I don't, she probably has to report to the police that I'm alone. "Yeah, my brother goes to college in Tampa. He's meeting me."

"Good." She waves me up the steps. "***sit right here behind me. Holler *** *** need anything."

"Thanks," I whisper, and as soon as I hit the seat, I fall asleep for the first time in two days.

CHAPTER 27

Even with only three hours of sleep, I'm feeling much better. The bus driver, Benia, is awesome, and I give her a giant hug when I leave. Now that I'm in Tampa, I think about calling Colby, but I know he'll just call our parents as soon as he hears from me. So instead, I take a city bus over to St. Pete.

At the drugstore near the bus stop, I find a pack of hearing aid batteries. The sticker says $14.97 for a pack, and my stomach sinks because all this time I had no idea they were so expensive. It costs a lot of money to have a hearing problem, which is really unfair considering it already stinks enough to not be able to hear.

I count my money. If I buy them, I'll only have $1.28 left, since the bus here from Tampa cost me $2. My palms sweat as I look around. I sneak two batteries out of the box and head for the exit, but with each step, I feel worse and worse. I stop, turn around, and go back. I grab the whole box and pay the full price, wondering what I'm going to do once I'm totally out of money. I need to figure things out fast.

―――――

I definitely didn't expect Bayview to be surrounded by a thick, black iron gate, and I wonder if it's to keep the blind students from wandering off campus. The diner across the street seems like a good place to sit and watch and hopefully figure out a way inside Bayview. It's only seven now, so it'll probably be a while before kids start showing up. I take a seat by the window.

"What *** I get ***?" a tall lady with red hair asks.

I pull what money I have left out of my pocket. "How much is a hot chocolate?"

"I'll have *** know that we're running *** special on hot cocoa. It's free when *** buy breakfast *** breakfast *** to be *** dollar today."

"I'm sorry. How many dollars is breakfast?"

She holds up one finger. "You're in luck."

Is there such a thing as luck? "Thank you. Then

can I have the French toast, please?" I point. "And if it's okay, I'm going to use the bathroom."

"Help yourself."

Before I go, I take out my notebook and on a blank page write *L U C K* in big letters. Is it something that just happens or something we create? Is it lucky that I'm here? I have no idea.

The pink bathroom stinks like roses, but it smells better than I do. I lock myself in the handicap stall and try to hurry so I can finish before anyone comes in. Because of my whole balance problem, I sometimes need the handrail next to the toilet, but since people don't know about my hearing, they think I'm just hogging up the handicap stall to be selfish. Some people are really mean about it too.

I undress and use a paper towel and soap to clean up. I rub the baby powder I brought into my scalp— a trick Mom showed me to get rid of greasy hair when you don't have time to wash it. Finally, I brush my teeth. It all feels so good.

By the time I get back to the booth, my hot chocolate's there, and I feel like I can do anything again. Except hear. Which is what I want to do, especially now because there are two boys close to my age sitting at the table next to me, one drinking hot cocoa and the other coffee. I imagine myself having a conversation with them. A year ago, I wouldn't have hesitated at all to say hi. But now, things are different.

Beep, beep. My other hearing aid's about to die, so I quickly change the battery. As soon as I'm done, I pick up my drink and blow on it, hoping no one noticed.

Out of the corner of my eye, I see things moving. I glance over and the two boys are signing. For real!

As excited as this makes me, it also bugs me, because I wish I knew sign. I'm pretty sure I can't get by just knowing *thank you, sunshine*, and *no brakes*. I'm not sure I'll be able to talk to people at Bayview today, if I even get on campus.

Just as I'm about to feel sorry for myself again, I think of Mr. Faro and the bike riding. He's so right. Today, I'm going to let go of the brakes once and for all.

One of the boys sees me staring and waves. I smile back and turn to watch the school while I eat. Pretty soon, I realize there's no way for me to get in on my own. All the kids have badges they swipe to open the gate, and they'll probably notice me if I try to tag along. But I have to try.

When the two boys leave the diner, I follow them across the street. The one who waved to me before looks back, and I turn and grab hold of the pink bougainvillea hanging from the iron fence, like it's the most beautiful thing I've ever seen.

He signs something to the other kid, who nods and keeps walking. The first one comes over to me, talking with his fingers, but I shrug and shake my head.

He pulls out a notebook and plops it down on the metal top of a sidewalk garbage bin, pulls out a pen, and writes, *I'm Eddison.*

I'm Rayne. Sorry if I was staring.

He laughs. Like a regular laugh out loud, not just an open mouth with no noise coming out. This surprises me more than it probably should. So does his smile. It's beautiful and . . . real. Like he's genuinely happy. I can't remember the last time I've been that happy. And I can't help wondering how he's so happy when he's obviously deaf.

He writes, *People always stare. No big deal.*

Now he reminds me of Troy. How come none of them care?

How come I do?

He writes again, *Do you live around here? I've never seen you.*

No. I just came to see your school.

His face scrunches in confusion.

I move my hair, so he can see my aids.

Yeah, I saw in the diner. Do you want to come here?

I didn't even know this place existed until a few weeks ago. Do you like it?

No. He laughs again. And he finishes with, *I love it.* I can tell he means it because it shows all over his face, especially in his eyes, which sparkle when he smiles.

I watch a group of girls inside the fence. They look like kids back home, hanging out, talking—maybe gossiping about crushes or parties or TV shows. Only, at home, they use words. Here, they sign. Either way, they're understood by everyone around them. Something I haven't experienced for a long time.

I'm not sure why I'm so surprised that this looks like a scene from my own school back home. I know the brochure showed this. And I watched the ChannelThis video a hundred times. But I guess I didn't really believe it.

Eddison writes, *You should take a tour. Where's your family?*

That's a good question. I bet they're scouring all of Orlando right now.

I write, *Long story. I ran away because my parents want me to get cochlear implants.*

He shakes his head super fast. *You don't need them. Just learn sign.*

Do you ever wish you could hear?

I can hear. I just listen differently than you.

I think on this. For a long time. I'm not sure why it hits me so hard. Maybe because I feel like an enormous jerk. It wasn't cool of me to assume that he's missing something, that he's—I don't know—defective because he's deaf. Honestly, it never occurred to me that it was possible for a deaf person to listen just as fully, to feel just as whole as a person without any hearing loss. That they don't feel bothered by their deafness. It reminds me of Helen Keller's thoughts on her disabilities.

Eddison taps me to get my attention, then writes, *I was born this way. I don't know anything different.* He points to his ears.

Maybe it's harder for me because I know what I'm missing. Or because my world's changing so fast, and I haven't had time to try to catch up, mostly because I've been worried about the surgery and fighting with Mom and Dad. I haven't had much time to really think about what this all means without being scared of it.

I miss the way music sounds, I write.

Ha! Deaf people are known for blasting music as loud as possible. We love the vibrations.

Sounds cool! But definitely not the same if you know what it should sound like. Before I even know what's happening, I tear up. With or without implants, I know now music will never, ever sound the same to me again. Last year it sounded perfect. And now the words are sometimes mumbled, but I can still hear some of them. By next year, though, I may not be able to hear any of it at all. And that makes me really angry.

Maybe Eddison senses my frustration because the smile drops from his face. He writes. *Were you born with hearing loss?*

I shake my head.

Look, the world wasn't made for people like us. Not gonna lie, that sucks! But at some point, you just decide to deal. And being here makes that easier. At least it has for me. He points to the school beyond the fence.

I write, *Can you sneak me in for the day?*

You picked a good day to come. We're giving a perfor-mance this morning for high school students who are study-ing ASL.

I point to *ASL* and shake my head, not sure what it means.

American Sign Language.

Oh, right. I knew that. *Cool. How do I get in?*

Follow me!

I gesture at my bags, not sure if I should lug them with me. He picks them up and walks me across the street and back into the diner. He signs with the red-haired lady who waited on me, and she says both out loud and in sign, "This *** my son. He wants me to hold *** bags. Rayne, is it?"

"Yes, and thank you," I say.

"I'm happy to put them *** *** office, but—"

Eddison shakes his head and makes more signs. He's getting super animated about something.

She signs and says, "He told me *** ran away. Aren't there people out there worried about ***?"

I close my eyes, knowing my parents are probably scared out of their minds. Colby too. And no matter how much I don't want those implants, my family at least deserves to know I'm okay.

I tear a piece of paper out of Eddison's notebook and write down Mom's cell number. "I get that you need to call. But can you at least give me a chance to see the school first? Maybe wait an hour?"

"I can't do that. But I do know there's a tour that starts *** fifteen minutes. I'll call over and put your name on *** list. Mr. Lazar is a great guy. He'll give you *** works. Your parents too."

My parents? I doubt they'd see Bayview as an option. I'm not even sure I do.

She hugs Eddison and signs while saying, "And you, *** going to be late again! We can't keep doing ***, Eds."

He kisses her cheek.

She smirks. "Now go on, both *** you."

I hug her too, even though she's basically a stranger. It just feels right.

"Hopefully I'll see you at *** show, Rayne."

Hopefully, when my family gets here, they won't put on a show of their own, with me in the starring role.

CHAPTER 28

The campus is way more awesome than the brochure shows. It's kind of old-fashioned looking, and my favorite part is the little beach area, where the sand is marshmallow-white and the water is see-through blue. Seriously, so clear. When Colby first got to the west coast of Florida, he was disappointed to learn that there are hardly any waves in the Gulf, but that's okay by me. It's probably better, actually. I could float on my board out there with my aids in and not even get my ears wet. My heart gives a little skip.

As the tour takes me from place to place—the dorms, the quad with tons of trees, the classrooms, and even the gym—I can picture myself here. It's frustrating, though, because I keep getting stuck in the back of the group, so I can't really hear, and I definitely can't understand Mr. Lazar's sign language. Neither makes me feel too bad, though, like it might have yesterday, because this school feels right in my gut, and I'm hopeful for the first time in a long time.

At least until Colby arrives. He's tearing across campus, headed for my group, and I stand stick-still. *Please, please don't make a scene.* I walk away from everyone, in case, and Mr. Lazar gives me a nod. Underneath a canopy of oak trees, Colby lifts me and practically squeezes the air of me. His cheek presses against mine, and I'm pretty sure it's wet.

Mr. Lazar strides over. Introducing himself to Colby, he hands each of us a water bottle. He stands in front of us and looks me right in the face, while signing too. "I'm glad you both could join us, and I'm happy to answer any questions you might have. Feel free to use my office to wait for your parents and to talk."

I sign, *Thank you.* It feels funny but really cool.

"See," Mr. Lazar says and signs. "You're a natural."

Colby shakes Mr. Lazar's hand and thanks him. We walk toward the front of the school, but instead of going in the office, we sit on the rim of a three-tiered stone fountain in the middle of campus.

Colby puts the cold water bottle on the back of his neck. "I'm sorry, Rayne."

"What?"

He turns to face me.

"No." I grab his arm. "Not *what* like I can't hear you. What are you sorry for? I'm the one who's caused all the trouble."

He shakes his head. "First, I promise to always speak so you can hear me. I know you've been going through a lot this last year, and I've let you down. I was so busy with my senior year stuff and getting ready for college, I hardly paid attention to you or your hearing problem. Even though I knew you and Mom were battling more than ever after I left, I still didn't try to help. The one time you asked my opinion, I screwed it up."

"You were honest. Even if I didn't like what you said, at least it was the truth. Maybe I needed to hear it."

"Yeah, but I shouldn't be giving you advice because I'm not you."

"You're the one person whose advice I need most. You're not Mom or Dad, so your opinion's not I-know-what's-best-and-that's-final. And you're not Jenika, who will take my side no matter what. I need you to tell me what you think."

"Man . . ." He bites his lip and shakes his head. "Fine, but I promise to pay better attention before I give it."

"Deal." I take a sip of water to cool down. "So how much trouble am I in?"

"No clue on the trouble. Mom and Dad are honestly just relieved that you're okay. Mom's feeling pretty guilty."

"For real?" My stomach sinks. I knew they'd be upset, but I've tried to block it all out.

"Yeah. She broke down in her classroom when Troy asked her why you were in Orlando."

"Wait, Troy?"

Colby nods.

"How did he even know?"

"He figured out you were posting pictures and did a search of some lake you were standing near. I guess there was a sign or something. At first, he thought you were with someone, but the comments on your page made him realize you were alone. He was worried."

I miss him more than I thought I would, even though I've only been gone a day. "How close are Mom and Dad to getting here?"

"They were in Orlando when the lady from the diner called them. I'm guessing they'll be here in the next thirty minutes or so."

I nod and try to picture myself with the implants, because surely that's what's going to happen when I get home.

Colby says, "So what do you think of this place?"

"It's pretty cool, I guess. I like how I feel here. But it doesn't matter. We both know I'm destined for implants."

Colby opens his mouth, closes it, and is quiet for another moment before he speaks. "It's awesome that this school exists. It seems like a great place for you. Especially if it means you won't have to get the implants." He wipes sweat from his forehead and takes off his button-down shirt, leaving him in a USF tee. He reaches for my backpack and shoves his shirt inside.

"But you said you thought I should get them."

"That was before I knew about Bayview. See, I shouldn't be giving advice when I don't know what I'm talking about. I haven't really seen the whole school, but it's got a good feeling to it, don't you think?"

I nod. "At home, school is so frustrating. And it's tiring. I have to strain super hard all day long to keep up, and then I'm so tired at the end that all I want to do is go home and sleep." I try to pull myself together, to be realistic. "But this place would probably be just as hard. I'd have to learn sign language, make new friends, ride a bus back and forth every weekend. So even if it does feel like it might be right for me . . . I don't know what to think." It's so hot; my hair is soaking wet underneath. I scoop it off my neck and hold it on top of my head for a few seconds.

Colby shoves his hand into the front pocket of my backpack and pulls out a hair tie.

I stare at him. He knows I don't wear my hair up anymore.

He aims it at me like a slingshot and shoots, but it hits my shoulder and drops into the fountain. We both reach for it at the same time, our hands touching under the water. *W-a-t-e-r*, I remember. Maybe my whole world could be here. Maybe it's about to burst open for me, like it did for Helen Keller. I smile at Colby, so grateful to have him for a brother. I take the hair tie and wind my hair into a ponytail. It feels good, and I'm not even embarrassed. "Thanks," I say.

He gives me a hug. "Why don't we walk around so I can see more?"

"There's a show that's about to start in the the-ater. Wanna go? My friend Eddison's in it."

"You've already made friends?"

"Yeah, it's pretty easy here."

He throws his arm around me. "I like it already."

———

Mr. Lazar's in the lobby when we walk in. "Rayne, I had them turn on the scrolling monitor for you. We do that when we have guests who are hard of hearing but can't yet sign."

Yet. It's a heavy word. I'm still the in-between. But not for long, because no matter what happens, I want to learn sign. It's actually beautiful to watch.

"Thanks," I say.

When we walk in, Eddison's onstage along with two other guys and three girls. They're dancing and mouthing the song "Love Me Tender," try-ing to keep up with the real lyrics being sung by an Elvis recording. It's extremely loud in here, but the routine's hilarious! Even Colby's cracking up. I wonder if Eddison's feeling the music in order to follow along.

I point. "That's Eddison."

Colby raises his eyebrows while nodding. "He's funny."

When they're done, Colby and I clap, but everyone else wiggles their fingers in the air. It takes me a second to realize that the performers wouldn't hear our applause, but they can see it. I love this.

Eddison's mom waves to me as she heads for the exit. "Couldn't *** seeing Eds, but I gotta scoot back *** work before *** fire me. Come *** *** bags whenever, okay, love?"

I nod and explain to Colby. He shakes her hand. "We'll be there soon. Thanks."

Next up is a girl who reminds me so much of a young Dr. Brandt, she could be her daughter. For a second, I wonder if she really is and that's why Dr. Brandt's studying stem cells. But I hear a whistle from the front row. An older man has his fingers in his mouth and his other hand's waving in the air. Next to him, a lady dries her eyes. I assume, since they're adults, that they must be her parents.

The girl's hot pink dress sparkles in the light. She's singing alone—signing, too—and her voice starts off so low I can't hear her, but the words are scrolling on the monitor. I turn on my music listening app and it pops up with the song's name: "Hear Me" by Kelly

Clarkson. I don't know the song, and it's a little slow at first, but a few seconds later, the girl's voice picks up and rages across the stage.

Through the auditorium.

Straight into my soul.

Her voice. The hands. It's like they're pleading to be heard right along with the lyrics about how lost she feels.

Each note pierces my body. My eyes well up, but I can't stop staring at her.

Her voice rises as she sings the lyrics about needing someone to hear her.

Colby reaches for my hand, and I use my other one to wipe my face. I'm not sure I've ever seen anything so amazing. It's not really even her voice, but the way she signs, so full of emotion. I have chills over my whole body. Does this girl feel exactly like me? I'm not sure I've met a single person who does. It's like we're wishing for the same things.

She finishes, and the entire place erupts—people on their feet, fingers and hands flying, but not me. I can't move. Not a single inch. Not until a hand touches my shoulder, and I turn to see Mom and Dad.

CHAPTER 29

In the lobby, my parents throw their arms around me. I hug them back, letting them feel all the sorry I've kept locked inside me. It's good to let it out.

Mom pushes me backward and inspects my face, my body. I expect her to yell and ask how I could have done this, but once she sees that I'm fine she pulls me in for another hug, her fingers running through my ponytail. My hearing aid screeches, so she pulls away.

Mr. Lazar shakes Dad's hand and then signs while speaking. "Nice to meet you. Rayne is a real sweetheart."

"That she is," Dad says.

I can't tell if he's being sarcastic or not. I don't think Mr. Lazar can either.

Mom points to Mr. Lazar's hands. "It's okay *** *** don't do that. *** *** us know sign language."

I'd never need to learn ASL if everyone spoke as clearly as Mr. Lazar does when he's near me. It's so nice to be able to hear every single word a person says.

"Yes, but we're an inclusive school, so we do it anyway. All the time." He chuckles. "Besides, it's a habit now."

Mom asks, "*** it easy *** learn?"

"It's a lot easier if you're fully immersed in it, but it's not too hard regardless, and messing up can be a lot of fun."

My cheeks grow hot as I imagine myself mixing up signs and kids laughing at me.

As if he can read my mind, Mr. Lazar says and signs, "We're not allowed to laugh at other people's mistakes here."

"Good to know," I say.

Mr. Lazar asks me, "Did you like that last girl on stage?"

"She blew me away."

Colby nods in agreement.

Mr. Lazar's fingers are flying. "She's a lot like you. Lost most of her hearing around ten, but she was raised oral, so she can speak."

"Well, I can't sing like that, so she's way better than me."

"Nah." He wags his finger. "We don't compare kids here either."

I glance at Mom to see what she thinks, but she looks out of it.

Dad puts his arm around her and says, "You *** kids here at *** deaf school that can hear?"

"A few," Mr. Lazar signs.

Mom's face is puzzled. "Why would *** want to come here then? Why not stay at *** regular school?"

"They can relax in their learning process here, since actual learning is all they have to focus on."

I think he's about to say more, but Mom cuts in, asking, "*** mean because *** don't do anything else here? No extracurriculars?"

"Quite the contrary—as you witnessed in there." He points toward the auditorium. "Plus, we have championship sports teams, academic teams, a Battle of the Books team, and more."

I ask, "Do you have student government?"

He raises his forearm and moves only his fist twice—like he's knocking on a door. "Yes."

I copy him, and he says, "Great, Rayne. You really are a natural."

Maybe I am. Maybe I could do this.

He turns to Mom. "To answer your question more fully about why—students like Rayne don't have to strain to hear in our classrooms, eliminating the main stressor that often holds them back academically. We start children here as young as three, but for those who come to us later, they're usually below grade level because parents and teachers in students' prior environments can't communicate in the ways that hard of hearing or deaf students need."

Mom literally gasps out loud. "Yes, that's *** my fear *** along. Rayne *** clearly falling behind, *** it's only going to get worse. *** *** why we're insisting *** *** cochlear implants."

"We have plenty of students with implants as well, but overall, it's not necessary. Deaf pride is strong here."

Mom straightens. "Rayne's not fully deaf. We feel *** implants *** her best hope *** carrying on a normal life."

Mr. Lazar replies, "I understand, but normal is relative."

"I'm sorry," Mom says. "I didn't mean *** offend."

"No offense taken."

"What about tuition, though?" Mom presses. "I assume a school this specialized must be costly."

"We're a public school," Mr. Lazar says. "Tuition, including our boarding facility, is free."

Mom finally seems to have run out of questions. Still, she looks kind of lost.

"Let me ask you this," says Mr. Lazar. "Rayne told me she began losing her hearing just over a year ago, but it's progressing quickly."

Mom nods.

Mr. Lazar says, "Hearing loss is just that, a loss. It can be just as traumatic as losing a loved one or a pet, and it takes time to move on. So I wonder, have you all really given yourselves, and especially Rayne, enough time to grieve her loss? Have you all had time to process it and accept it before making any big life-altering decisions?"

His words feel like a blanket. They soothe my racing thoughts. They are truer than anything I've heard in probably forever. I haven't had time to deal with my hearing loss, and already I'm being forced to deal with the thought of implants. I wonder if Mom feels the same, because she's seriously crying right here in the lobby. And she hugs me, tighter than ever.

Mr. Lazar signs and says, "I'm sure this is a lot to digest, but if you're interested, we're happy to discuss our admissions process, and we always have room for new students."

"But wait," I say. "Even if I did come here, how would I learn? I can't hear well, but I can't sign either."

"Students in your case are assigned a one-on-one interpreter for the first semester, while they immerse themselves in ASL. We recommend, even if a family lives close by, that students utilize our boarding school. There's no better way to pick up sign quickly than to spend after-school hours hanging out with friends, being teens. Socializing would help you learn in record time."

That part sounds fun, a whole dorm filled with kids, but it's also scary. Living on my own.

Mom physically shudders.

It's like Dad knows Mom's had enough. He reaches out his hand to Mr. Lazar. "Thank *** *** *** time. And *** keeping Rayne safe *** we got here. We appreciate ***."

"Not a problem at all," he signs. "Glad to have met you."

Colby puts my bags in Dad's car while the rest of us order food at the diner across from Bayview.

Mom's swirling her water with a straw. "I'm not going to even ask *** why, Rayne. *** pretty sure we all know. But didn't *** realize how dangerous it *** to run away? What *** something had happened to ***? Where did *** *** sleep?"

No need to give all the details and freak her out more. "I slept on a bus. I *had* to talk to Dr. Brandt for myself. I couldn't do the surgery without trying everything I could first."

She asks, "But that's what I don't get. Don't *** think we did that?"

I don't answer. They already know what I think about that.

Colby sits next to me.

Dad grabs my hands across the table. "I've *** trying *** put myself *** your shoes."

I change the background noise setting on my aids since the diner's loud.

Dad keeps talking. "Running away *** drastic, not to mention scary, but I do apologize that we weren't taking *** as seriously as you needed us to. I understand now the desperation you felt. We're all struggling *** deal with this quickly and make sure

*** stay on top of school and other stuff as usual, but perhaps we could *** handled things differently. Perhaps we all should have slowed down. I'm really sorry, pumpkin."

I can't believe he's apologizing. I completely lose it. Through sobs, I spill everything, because I can't hold it in any longer. "I'm sorry too. I've been lying for a long time. I've been telling you my hearing's not that bad. Pretending I know what everyone's saying and that I don't care when people laugh at me for guessing wrong. I pretend I have a lot of friends and make excuses for not hanging out with people. I pretend to be fine at student government meetings. I pretend that I don't worry what other people think of me. I tell myself that stem cell transplants are going to be ready in the next year. I told myself that it was okay to run away because I could handle myself. But they're lies. Every single one of them. And you guys knew it all along, but I kept on lying. I bet even Jenika knows I've been pretending. My hearing is worse than I admitted. And I'm sorry. I really am. But I'm so afraid of those implants." I put my head on the table and cry into a napkin.

Colby drapes his arm around me and, after a few seconds, gives me a nudge, like he's letting me know he's got my back. He asks Mom and Dad, "*** *** *** school, ***?"

I pick my head up, so I can hear better and see his lips.

He goes on, "I took part of the tour with Rayne. This seems like a good place. Worth a shot at least, and I'm close by."

I'm so glad Eddison's mom gave us a booth in the back corner because Mom practically yells, "How *** someone just send *** kid away? She's only twelve."

Colby stops her. "Mr. Lazar said they bus kids home every weekend. Some as far as Key West."

Mom sniffles.

We all sit in silence. My mind's racing.

Eventually, Mom takes a deep breath and asks clearly, "What do *** think *** *** school, Rayne?"

"I like that I wouldn't have to get implants!" I blurt, but I instantly wish I could take it back. She's asking my opinion for once. I need to be serious and fully honest.

Colby laughs, and Mom gives him a you're-not-helping look. She turns back to me, meeting my eyes.

"Help me understand, Rayne. I want to *** where *** coming from on this."

If she's for real, then this is everything to me. So I say exactly how I feel. The truth I didn't even know was inside me. "I *am* afraid of the surgery," I say. "And of all the other possible side effects I've already talked to you about. But I don't think that's really what we're fighting over. Mostly . . ." I sniff and try to look at them, but I can't. "Mostly, I don't think you like me like this. You want to fix me, because I'm not a perfect student anymore. Or the daughter you used to be proud of. And the truth is, *I* don't even like me anymore. I haven't liked me in a long time. But being here, I feel like maybe I could, even if I can't hear. I don't feel like I have to hide here. I could just be me—broken ears and all."

Mom stands and tells Colby to trade places with her, and now she's sitting next to me, holding me. Rocking. She tries to talk, but I cut her off.

"Maybe I'd hate it if I came to Bayview. Maybe I wouldn't want to leave you guys, or Jenika, or Troy. But maybe I ended up here for a reason. Do you think sometimes things happen that way?"

Dad says, "We've had hours *** *** car while searching *** you to discuss some things. *** hearing loss came on so fast. Maybe *** *is* another answer besides implants or stem cells. Even if it's not this school."

"Do you mean it?" My eyes, my face, my whole body are begging.

Mom nods. "I'll call and *** the surgery. We all need time to process ***."

I think I heard her right, but I'm not sure. "You'll call and what?"

"Cancel," she says. "I'll cancel the surgery, for now."

I throw one arm around her and reach for Dad's hand. "Thank you," I whisper. "And I'm sorry."

Dad says, "My girl!"

Mom cups my face in her hands and puts her face close to mine. "Rayne, *** sorry too. I'm sorry if you felt I was trying to fix you because *** weren't good enough anymore. You will always be good enough. Better than good enough. You are an amazing daughter with a kind soul and a penchant *** helping others. You're a lover of *** ocean and people. It hurt my heart to see you pulling away from all *** things that made you *you*. I just wanted you to feel like yourself again. I thought implants would do that, even if *** couldn't see it right away. Maybe I was wrong. This is a new you, and you're still wonderful. We just all need to be patient while you find your way to shine again. However we *** decide down the road."

I want to believe them. I mean, they've always been honest, even when I didn't like what they said. So for now, I go with it. Relief floods me.

———

We say bye to Colby, and I climb into the backseat. Comfortable. Safe. Happy. On the highway, we pass a GreenFox bus, and I wonder if Pink Headphone Girl is on it. I hope not. I hope by now she is sleeping safely somewhere. I hope that, like me, she's found what she was looking for, and more than anything, I hope she won't need to run ever again.

CHAPTER 30

When I finally go to school the following week, Mr. Grady asks for volunteers to present their biography projects. I haven't prepared for it. I haven't written detailed words in my notebook to memorize. But none of it freaks me out. I've totally got this. I raise my hand. Helen's been on my mind nonstop anyway.

"I wanted to do my report on R-Jarrow. I mean, who's more influential than that, right?" Some people laugh. It's a good start. "Turns out, someone else was influential too. I knew a little about Helen Keller. I knew that she was both deaf and blind and that she was famous. But I didn't really *know* about her. You guys, she totally kicked butt! In just about everything she did. Do me a favor for a second. Close your eyes and cover your ears."

People start to do it, but I yell, "Wait! In just a second. When you do this, imagine your whole day, start to finish, without being able to see or hear. For real. Like, getting up with an alarm you can't see or hear, so maybe it shakes your bed. Trying to get into the shower, but not hearing water. You get it. Do that for a few seconds."

Surprisingly, they do.

Most of them hear me when I say, "Okay, what do you think you'd miss the most?"

One boy says, "*** never know if *** girl *** cute enough *** date *** not."

Mr. Grady interjects, "Please take this seriously."

Adam joins in, loudly. "He's not wrong, but okay, probably music."

I guess he and I have one thing in common in this universe. "Sure," I say. "That's a big one for me too."

"Honestly," Beth says, "*** not sure I'd leave *** house *** again."

A few kids nod.

"Exactly," I say. "It's really hard to function in a world that doesn't usually accommodate you." I'm glad she gets it. "Helen Keller not only left her house all the time, but she traveled the world. She became an advocate for people with disabilities—we learned all about the American Civil Liberties Union this year. Helen was a founder of that. But she did a whole lot more. She used her words to publicly fight against racism, war, and poverty, and to fight for women's rights. When people challenged her, she never backed down. She actually welcomed it. She debated with facts but also threw in emotional things that made people think in new ways. If you ever read her writing, you'll see she was incredibly smart. Education meant everything to her, and she won the respect of leaders all over the world."

Beth asks, "*** could she *** educated if she couldn't hear *** see?"

I'm not sure I heard her right, but I'm not about to guess on this again. "How? Is that what you asked?"

Beth nods.

"Great question." I tell them all about her teacher and the finger spelling and how she felt people's faces to understand words as they spoke. That last part takes even more bravery if you ask me. I think I'd be embarrassed, but Helen cared more about learning and interacting with people than she cared about what anyone thought of her. "And it worked. She was brilliant. That's because she never gave up."

I don't plan to give up either. There's a whole world out there as long as I'm brave enough to face it. Mom and Dad are considering Bayview, but we still have a lot of questions. All of us promised we'd make the important decisions with lots of talking and especially listening, so even if I don't get my way in the end, I'm thankful for that. I still don't want the implants, like at all, but I've been texting with Maddie from the support group, and at least I'm not *as* afraid of CIs as I was before. Who knows how I'll feel if I ever go fully deaf. Maybe I'd change my mind about them.

Mr. Grady says, "Great. Now *** *** question."

I had no idea he'd do this, but I've read the book on Helen cover to cover a few times now, so I'm pretty sure I can answer anything he throws my way, as long as I can hear what he's saying.

I'm surprised when he asks a personal question instead of something about her specifically. "Why did *** choose Helen Keller?"

I think on this, because I didn't really mean to pick her. It just happened. "Most of you know I've been having hearing trouble lately. That's kind of what led me to Helen Keller. In the beginning, I didn't like her. She seemed too perfect, almost made up. You know? I mean, who could be such a great person, always positive, when she couldn't see or hear anything? I didn't get it. I thought maybe writers made her seem more cheerful or more important than she really was. I guess I wanted to find out if that was all a bunch of lies, because I was telling lies myself—pretending that my hearing loss was no big deal, and sometimes even pretending nothing was wrong with me at all."

Even Adam's paying attention. I keep going.

"So maybe I picked Helen to prove she was a liar too, or a phony, or not as great and accepting of her disabilities as everyone said, because I didn't get how she could be okay with all that. How she could be okay with who she was and what happened to her. I know that's mean, but it's what I hoped I'd learn. Except it turned out she totally *was* okay with herself. And sure, she was frustrated a lot—which I get—but she believed in herself and in what she was capable of. And maybe I can do the same someday."

I'm definitely ready to be done, but Jenika raises her hand. I shake my head at her, but she asks loudly, "What's something you learned about Helen that surprised you? You know, besides what you already covered."

I think for a second and say, "I read a letter Helen wrote to a friend where she said a lot of thoughtless people assumed that, just because she couldn't hear or see, her world must have been pretty dull. Like without color and context and stuff. But she gave an example about how she could appreciate the beauty of a flower—not because of how it looked, obviously, but how it felt in her hands. Every single petal, leaf, and stem. Its scent, its texture. Most people look at a flower and think it's pretty, but how many actually touch it? Explore it? She enjoyed the world in a powerful way, a different way than what I'm used to, and I love that."

The truth is, my favorite quote of Helen's is something she wrote to her friend about the stars. She said even though she'll never be able to physically see gold-dusted stars in the sky, that doesn't keep stars from shining brightly inside her. I can't imagine never having seen Delphinus or even Arcturus— but maybe it's their story that inspires more than their shining. "So yeah. It took me a long time to understand where Helen was coming from, but she was fierce and unapologetic and always wanted to know more." And maybe someday, like her, I'll stop feeling less than anyone else. For now, I'm definitely done hiding, at least.

Helen wasn't perfect. Neither am I, but I think both of us are pretty brave.

I look at Troy across the room. He gives me a double thumbs up and grins at me. The minnows still scurry in my stomach whenever I see him, and I hope that feeling never stops.

Mr. Grady nods. "Excellent report, Rayne!" The whole class claps. For me.

———

After the next SGA meeting, I text Sabrina. *Can we talk?*

She meets me out in front of the school. We sit on a bench under the flagpole.

She asks, "What's up?"

"I probably shouldn't have run for president this year. The truth is, I can't hear in the meetings. I have no clue what we're supposed to be doing for the Harvest Fest." Today's meeting was just as bad as every other. At least now I can admit it to Mom. I know she'll help me, if I want, but this is a better solution. "I think you should be president."

"No ***. Not happening. *** won fair and square. Your speech *** your ideas were amazing. And you've been killing it with the Harvest Fest."

I guess my letter was pretty awesome. We've had

over six thousand dollars in donations so far, with more coming in every day. "Thanks, but I honestly can't do this job the right way. I'll just help you."

She thinks for a while. "*** really can't?"

I'm glad I don't have to pretend anymore. "I really can't."

"Fine." She grabs my arm. "***, *** about this? We can be co-presidents *** rule *** school together."

"Co-presidents . . ." I let that thought settle. It's actually perfect. Almost everything finally is.

———

Mom wakes me up early on Saturday, but neither Lucky nor I want to get out of bed.

Mom shakes me again. "Get dressed, *** come to *** living room. I have *** surprise."

Ten minutes later, I walk into a room full of everyone I love—like truly everyone. Colby's still at school, but Sierra's here and has him on FaceTime. Plus, all my usual friends are here, and Mr. Faro.

I pat my hair down, hoping I don't look like a mess, even though I feel like I am. "What's going on?"

Mom gestures to the one person I don't know.

"This *** Mrs. B***ducci. For *** next few weeks, she's going to be teaching *** to sign. We'll meet here for an hour or so once a week, and anyone who can't make it in person can join virtually."

The teacher signs while saying, "I'll record the sessions, so you can rewatch them online as often as you need."

Lucky nuzzles against my leg.

I look around the room. No one says April Fool's or anything. I press my hands to my face to keep myself together. I can't believe they'd all do this for me. "For real?"

Mr. Faro holds up his fist and knocks the air twice, the sign for yes.

Troy does the same. I guess he's already got a head start too.

I squeeze my eyes tight and let it sink in. I knew ASL wouldn't help me much if I was the only one learning it, so this—having all these people here for me—it's more than I could ever ask for. I really am the luckiest.

CHAPTER 31

Mom got Colby and me matching Christmas jammies, and even though we protested, we're now sitting in front of the tree for a photo. My shirt is green with red lettering that says *Naughty* and an arrow pointing to my left. She makes Colby sit to my left. His red shirt with green lettering says, *Oh, deer!* with antlers on top of the *d*. Lucky's decked out in an elf dog costume that, from the front, makes it look like she has arms that are planted on her front leg hips. It's all sooooo corny! But Colby and I laugh and try to have fun with it because it's just Mom being Mom.

Dad brings in a tray of hot cocoa, even though it's ninety degrees outside. He turned the air down last night to make it feel "wintery."

Just when I thought we were done with gifts, Colby hands Mom and Dad an envelope.

Mom tears it open. "What's ***?" A smile breaks across her face, and she hands it to Dad while she gets up to give Colby a hug. "All As and Bs. I'm *** proud *** how hard you worked."

Dad hugs Colby too. "Yes, really proud of you."

Mom takes it back from Dad and hangs it on the fridge, which bites since she hasn't hung anything of mine since my grades dropped.

Dad must notice my face. "What's wrong?"

Since we've all promised to listen to each other more, I tell them the truth.

Mom replies, "Sweetie, last spring *** begged me to stop putting them up. Begged. Don't *** remember?"

"Yeah, but I'd been begging you for years, and you never listened. Then, all of a sudden, my grades slip and *bam*, no more report card on the fridge."

"I can see *** *** think it was related, but I promise *** it wasn't. We were having Colby's graduation party, and I knew you hated me showing people, *** I just didn't put it up. But *** didn't put Colby's up either."

"True." I remember now. Maybe I'm being overly sensitive lately. "Sorry for thinking the worst."

Dad laughs. "You really can tell us things. I hope you'll trust in that again."

"Thanks," I say.

Mom hands me one last thing. It's wrapped in a shirt box, so I assume it's more clothes, but I'm surprised to see a thick envelope when I open the lid.

There's a logo in the corner that says *Bayview School for the Deaf and Blind.*

Dad says, "Hurry up. It came three days ago, and I almost opened it myself—I'm dying to know."

Mom and Dad did a ton of research on the school. They even talked to the cochlear surgeon about it. We all agreed that Bayview seems like something we should at least try before we make a drastic change to my body. Mr. Lazar was especially convincing and promised Mom she'll be able to check in on me as often as she wants. He secretly told me to be patient with her because it would be a lot at first, but she'd be fine once she knew I was settled.

I rip the envelope and pull out a letter. "I got in!" For a quick second I feel like I'm back on my surfboard and the octopus is lurking below. "I mean, Mr. Lazar basically told me I'd get in since I met all the criteria, but now it's all . . . real." I'm happy. But whoa, it's a lot to take in.

Dad teases, "Mr. Lazar should be canonized a saint after dealing with your mother—"

Mom shoves him. "*** not that bad."

Dad and Colby both nod their heads.

"But . . ." Mom says.

I brace myself.

"Don't give me that look." Mom laughs. "My only *but* is that *** don't have to go *** you don't want to. It's *** choice."

My choice. *Mine.* I can hardly believe it. I hug them. Then I hug them again. I'm not sure I'll let go for a while.

———

New Year's Day is a great time for a send-off. New beginnings, as Jenika says. It was her idea to throw me the going-away party, but it was Troy's idea to have it at the beach. Even Lucky's here, sound asleep on the sand. The pavilion's decked out with blue and yellow streamers—Bayview's colors—and I'm surprised how much this feels like old times.

Honestly, this party makes me wonder if going to Bayview is a mistake. Things have been so good at home and even at school lately. But I fought hard to be able to try it, and I need to go.

I push all my worries out of my head for now because I only have two days left before I leave. All my favorite people are here, so I soak everything in. It feels great to be around them all and to not care one bit about my ears.

———

Everyone watches the sunset together, and Mrs. Jackson brings out the cake she made. When we're done eating, Troy sucks in helium from a balloon and squeaks, "Want to go for a paddle?"

My hands are sweating as soon as he says it. Winter brings the best waves to Florida, and today they're nugs—not huge but perfect for surfing. Terrible for just hanging out, though.

Troy grabs my hand and says, "Come on, we're going to stay shallow, I promise."

Colby adds, "You've got this."

I turn toward the ocean. I miss surfing so much. I don't want to give it up forever. Octopus or no octopus, I'm ready to try again. Let go of the brakes. I hand my aids to Colby and tuck the board under my arm.

Troy squeezes my fingers. We've been officially dating for a few months now, but my stomach still gets fluttery every single time he does this. It makes me miss him already. I rock forward on my toes and smile, and we walk toward the water. I wasn't sure he would want me to leave, but he was all for it. Then I worried that things would change, that we'd go back to just being friends, but so far, they're better than ever. Plus, now he'll have lots more time for his video game streaming. His one thousand current subscribers will be happy, and I bet he'll have a sponsor really soon.

He takes the board from under my arm and sets it in the water. I'm extra careful climbing on, and when I'm finally sitting, I hold tight to the sides—wobbling and shaking. Troy holds the board steady, one hand on it and his other arm across my legs like a seatbelt. I'm sure he's yelling so I can hear well, but with the full moon, I can read his lips perfectly. "*** excited about school?"

I definitely am. Eddison put me in a group chat, so I've met some other kids too, and they've made me feel a lot better—though who knows if I'll like Bayview as much as they do? "Yeah, but I'm nervous too. What if it's a mistake? What if I hate it?"

"*** really cute girl once told me, right here on this very beach, that *** never know what you're meant to *** until you try."

Wow, I do remember saying that.

"Besides," he says. "If you don't like it, then *** come home. No big deal, right?"

The waves are rocking the board, and I'm still gripping it tightly, so Troy lets the current carry us back to the shallow. He climbs on the opposite end of my board and faces me, our feet gripping the sand with our toes to steady us. This is much better.

I say, "I mean, I couldn't just quit on a whim. I caused enough trouble to get in, you know?" I feel like I ended up at Bayview that day for a reason, and it's up to me to make it work now.

"I know. You always try your hardest at everything you do. But I *** a feeling *** parents will be fine if it's not working ***."

He's not wrong. Mom and Dad—but especially Mom—have told me multiple times that I can come home if I need to. It's hard to be spontaneous—to totally let go of the brakes—but I do believe that whatever happens, everything will work out.

Troy stands and straddles the board for a second

while yanking on the Velcro of his bathing suit pocket. "I *** something for ***, Star Girl."

The minnows in my belly are doing flips. I love it when he calls me that. He sits again and hands me something shiny that glistens in the full moonlight. It's a necklace with a silver eyeball pendant dangling. "Arcturus!" I snort-laugh, and my smile travels all the way down to my heart. "I love it!"

"If *** get lonely in St. Pete, *** can always text me, or *** can look up and find *** eyeball, because I'll probably be looking at it too. You know, whenever it's visible."

It's the sweetest thing ever. "Then I'll be looking every single night, pretending it's there even when it's not."

He clips it around my neck and kisses my cheek. That's when I practically fall over. But just like he promised, Troy loops his fingers in mine and steadies us, while the stars wink above.

———

I flop onto Jenika's bed while Lucky and Putter snuggle on the shaggy purple rug. Jenika's tossing her volleyball in the air.

I say jokingly, "Who's going to keep you from getting kicked off the team next year if I stay at Bayview?"

"*** *** already looking *** excuses not to go?"

"Maybe." And it's partly true. I can't get my nerves to stop racing.

"Don't worry about me." She slaps the ball like I've seen her do in warm-ups. "I stuck it out last season, but there's no way I'm playing *** Coach A again. I'm doing *** club team next fall instead. At least till high school. No way your dad would hire *** bad coach, right?"

"Hmm." I tap my chin, pretending to be deep in thought before I playfully reply, "Maybe my dad will bring Coach A to Sawgrass. I could ask him."

Jenika waves an envelope. "Right. *** maybe I'll just toss *** present in the trash then."

I laugh and grab it from her "For me? You shouldn't have." When I open it, two R-Jarrow concert tickets land in my lap. "Are you serious?"

"She'll be here in April. And since you'll be home on the weekends . . ."

We jump up and down together. R-Jarrow's full album, *Unchained*, dropped in October. Since then, I've looked up all the lyrics to put with the music, and you know what? The album is totally her best ever. The concert will be amazing, even if I have to turn my aids all the way down. I'm not missing it.

I squeeze Jenika tightly, and as soon as we step apart, I lose it, crumbling onto her bed.

"Whoa." She sits next to me.

"I'm going to miss you." Understatement. I'm not sure how I'll survive without her.

"What are *** talking about?" She throws her closet door open, grabs an armful of clothes, and tosses them on the bed. "I'm coming with ***, remember?"

I laugh. "I wish you were for real. It would make this a lot less scary."

She jumps onto the pile of clothes. "I'm *** jealous about *** dorm. Imagine if we *** roommates."

"That's what college is for."

"True!" She flips over. "We should apply to schools *** California. I hear it's amazing out ***. Lots of cute surfers. But *** probably still be with Troy. Or Eddison." She raises her eyebrows.

"What?" I shove her off the bed. "No way. Eddison is a friend. Look what Troy gave me." I lean over to show her the necklace.

"*** my gosh. It's so . . ." Her face squishes. "Ugly!"

I smack her.

"Okay," she says. "It's interesting. Better?"

"It's perfect!"

"*** two can name *** first son Arcturus."

I throw a handful of clothes at her. "Not funny." And just like that I'm sad all over again.

Jenika pops onto her knees. "I'm sorry. I *** kidding."

"It's not that." I grab Lucky and put her on my lap. "This, us hanging out, is what I'm going to miss. And my dog. What if I don't make any friends? What if no one wants to talk to me because I can't sign? What if I don't find a friend there as good as you are?"

"First of all, *** ridiculous." She sits next to me. "Everyone there is going to love ***. How could they not? You're already talking to people anyway. And second, *** better not be anyone *** like me because I'm irreplaceable."

I laugh. "True. You are." And I mean it. "I don't think I'll ever be able to thank you enough for sticking by me all this time. For never making fun of me and my ears or getting frustrated with me. For covering for me, especially at school, when you knew I didn't hear something right." I shake my head. "I really don't think I can go without you."

"Please. It'll be like I'm *** because I expect *** to FaceTime me every single night, so I can meet your friends. And if *** don't like Eddison that way, I'll snatch him up. *** should bring him home with *** one weekend, so I can meet him in person."

I roll my eyes.

"Seriously. Bayview is the right place for you. We both know it." She puts her hand on mine.

"Yeah. It is." I'm going to miss her, Troy, my family, and even Mr. Faro, but thinking of their support brings a smile to my face. I'm actually getting the best of everything. I can go to a school where I'll feel good, be able to understand things and learn, and hopefully make even more friends, but I can still see everyone here on weekends too. Luck is a pretty cool thing.

CHAPTER 32

The car is packed, and Lucky's pouting on the couch. She hates suitcases. It's like she knows. I try super hard not to cry when I say bye and remind her that I'll only be gone a few days a week. Somehow, I don't think it makes her feel better. "I know, girl. I feel you. Maybe I'll be able to sneak you in my bag sometime." I give her one last kiss and head out the door.

We have to make a stop at Dr. James's office for an updated audiogram. I guess it's Bayview's rule.

Colby knows how much I hate these checkups. He says, "Sure *** don't want me to come with ***?"

It's better if he leaves for Tampa now, so he can drop his own stuff off before he meets us at Bayview to move me in later. We're planning a beachnic on campus with Eddison, some of his friends, and my parents afterward.

Before Mom and Dad drive home.

That part still seems so weird.

I say to Colby, "I'm good, but thanks."

He gives me a hug before getting in his car and leaving. It's going to be nice having him close by again.

———

Dr. James asks, "How's my favorite patient?" He gives me a fist bump and shakes Mom's and Dad's hands.

"I'm great!"

He sits behind his desk and points for us to sit too. "And how about her parents?" He looks at Mom and Dad.

"Better ***," Mom says.

He opens my file. "It's good to see you all smiling."

Dad nods. "We couldn't agree more."

Mom squeezes my shoulder. I know my going off to Bayview won't be easy for her. But she's come a long way lately. We both have.

"So." Dr. James slaps his desk. "You ready, Rayne?"

My chest is so full. With happiness. Happiness that my parents would do this for me. That they're letting me go. That they love me.

Like Colby, Mom knows how much I hate this part, and she kisses my cheek. But when I climb inside the testing box, for the first time ever it doesn't make me feel stupid. This time, I know my ears just are what they are. Even if my hearing is worse today than the last time I was here, there's no rush to figure things out. There's no reason to guess answers or pretend I can hear. Finally, I can just be me.

Dr. James seals the door behind me, and though I'm surrounded by the same hole-filled walls and that creepy Mickey Mouse–like mask—seriously, he needs to get rid of it—I don't feel even a tiny bit of shame. My ears might be broken, but I'm not.

AUTHOR'S NOTE

At the age of sixteen, I was diagnosed with progressive sensorineural hearing loss. I'm not sure what prompted my parents to take me for testing, since I don't remember struggling to hear. They say they just knew. I guess, in hindsight, I recall not being able to hear lyrics very well, so I'd blast the radio or put my ear right up to the speaker to figure them out. And I was often laughed at for mispronouncing words in conversations. But I didn't *feel* different back then. Honestly, I assumed TVs, radios, and movies were difficult for anyone to understand clearly.

It's probably important to mention that as a kid—and truthfully, even now—I hated standing out. I hated being different. In the 1980s, a time when many disabilities were not widely understood or accepted, kids laughingly tossed around offensive words regarding anyone who was different. So I did all I could to deny my hearing loss. Things changed in college when I knew for certain my hearing was declining. At that point, an audiologist recommended hearing aids. When I finally got my first hearing aids at age twenty, they felt gigantic. It felt like the whole world was staring at them. Not to mention, the aids gave me constant, intense headaches from all the new noise my brain was trying to process. After two weeks, I tucked them away in a drawer.

As my hearing continued deteriorating over the years, I quit my teaching job, avoided most social situations, and eventually purchased the smallest hearing aids possible—upgrading to newer aids any time I could afford the $5,000 price tags. The aids definitely amplified sounds, but they never helped me decipher actual words. In essence, I could hear lots of things loudly but never clearly. And I felt stuck. Always! Since I didn't sign, I didn't fit in with the Deaf community, yet I was legally deaf and trying to navigate a hearing world that wasn't built to accommodate someone like me. My frustration, at times, turned to mild depression, and hiding from the world became my coping mechanism.

In writing this book, I learned much about my own loss. Despite living with it every day, I could never quite put into words what I was experiencing—and I needed to understand it fully in order to make this book as authentic as possible. So I consulted with my audiologist turned dear friend, Dr. Fred Rahe. I wanted to accurately portray on the page what Rayne could and could not hear. I wasn't sure exactly which words to omit from the dialogue. You'd think I'd know what I can hear and what I miss, but that has never been the case. I knew I had trouble with softer letters and soft vowels, including sounds like *s, sh, th, n,* and *m,* but if someone were to say a sentence and ask me to repeat only the words I knew for certain that I'd heard, I wouldn't be able to do it. Dr. Rahe explained the medical phenomenon of auditory closure, a normal occurrence with hearing loss. If I'd written only what Rayne was technically able to hear, the story would have been unintelligible. Since Rayne is able to figure out sentences through cues and clues, I instead used asterisks judiciously. After all, Rayne's brain does think it's actually hearing the words, and therefore the dialogue in this book represents her *understanding* rather than what she actually hears.

One thing I can attest to is that auditory closure is exhausting—both mentally and physically, especially as my hearing continued to decline and hearing aids stopped benefiting me. My audiologist frequently brought up the option of cochlear implants. Much like Rayne, I was terrified of them—terrified of surgery in general, terrified of how they'd look, terrified of how people would treat me, but mostly I was terrified of them not working. The majority of people who get cochlear implants lose their residual hearing. That meant if the surgery was unsuccessful—as it is for some people—whatever natural hearing I had left would also be gone. I'd be completely deaf. For me, a little hearing was better than no hearing at all, so I clung to hearing aids for as long as I could.

Unlike Rayne, I had many years to come to terms with my loss. Mine was much slower than hers. I don't think there's a truer line in the book than when Mr. Lazar tells Rayne and her family that they deserve time to process and grieve the loss of Rayne's hearing. It took me years to grieve my loss, and while I wish that accepting my disability had been a faster process for me, I'm glad the choice to get an implant or not was my own.

Through my research, I met a guy in a support group who had been bilaterally implanted (with CIs in both ears). Surgery didn't work for him, so he had the CIs explanted and reimplanted a few years later.

Once again, the surgery was unsuccessful. This man was angry and bitter about his experience, and while it scared me, I also appreciated his honesty. I knew, for certain, I'd never be able to have CI surgery until I got to a place where I could accept the possibility of an unsuccessful operation. I needed to be sure that if it didn't work for me, I wouldn't live the rest of my life angry and resentful.

That same group led me to a consultation with an amazing surgeon, Dr. Fred Telischi, at the University of Miami. I told myself I was only meeting with him for Rayne's benefit . . . the story's benefit. It was a lie I believed, just like Rayne believed the lie that her hearing was fine. The truth of it, though, is that meeting Dr. Telischi changed everything for me. He answered my questions with fact-based science and calmed my fears. By that time, the hearing in my left ear was at only 8 percent, and after much soul-searching, I knew that losing 8 percent versus potentially gaining any hearing and clarity was a worthwhile gamble, so I decided to go ahead with a unilateral (one ear) implantation. Surprisingly, the decision alone brought immense peace.

I'm grateful to have a supportive family and friend group who embraced my choice. They never pushed me one way or the other. They never saw me as flawed, even though I saw myself that way for far too long. And during my recovery, they were with me every step of the way.

My surgery was a huge success, but my hearing will never be perfect. In quiet situations, my hearing is now up to 100 percent word recognition. In louder settings, it's around 72 percent. The clarity of words is incredible—something I've missed for the last thirty years. I still cannot decipher lyrics to songs well, and I still use captioning on my TV. Large groups and noisy places will forever be challenging environments for me. But for the most part, as of this writing—one and a half years post-surgery—I've gained back the independence I lost so long ago.

I wrote this book before I had my cochlear implant, but ironically, it sold just two weeks after surgery. Fate? Luck? Who knows? But I'm glad I'm able to share Rayne's story with the world.

For those of you who feel you don't fit in in either a hearing world or a deaf one, you are not alone. Reach out to support groups. Talk to people in similar situations. But remember, your journey is your own. No better, no worse—just different.

RESOURCES FOR THE DEAF AND HARD OF HEARING

American Sign Language (ASL):

Language First
https://language1st.org

General Support and Information:

American Speech-Language-Hearing Association
(ASHA)
https://www.asha.org

American Society for Deaf Children
https://deafchildren.org

Hearing Loss Association of America
https://www.hearingloss.org

Laurent Clerc National Deaf Education Center
https://clerccenter.gallaudet.edu

National Association of the Deaf
https://www.nad.org

Cochlear Implant Technology:

Cochlear Implant Awareness Foundation
http://www.ciafonline.org

QUESTIONS FOR DISCUSSION

1. Why is Rayne so against getting cochlear implants? Why are her parents convinced it's the right move?

2. Mr. Faro encourages Rayne to "let go *** *** brake, and enjoy *** ride." What do you think letting go of the brakes means for Rayne? What are some examples of her doing this?

3. Throughout the book, Jenika remains supportive of Rayne as she struggles with her hearing loss. How does Rayne, in turn, support Jenika as a friend?

4. How does Rayne's hearing loss change how she's able to interact with friends? Give two or three examples.

5. Why is Rayne reluctant to spend more time with Troy, even though she likes him a lot? Why is it hard for her to believe that Troy likes her as she is?

6. Describe a couple of different ways that Rayne approaches her parents about why she doesn't want implants. Would you use any of her strategies to have a hard conversation?

7. Why does Rayne try to see Dr. Brandt in person? Do you think she makes the right choice?

8. Rayne works really hard to become SGA president. But eventually, she realizes she can't do the job on her own. Can you think of a time when you worked hard for something and achieved it? What about a time when you realized you needed to step back or ask for more help?

9. At Bayview, Mr. Lazar tells Rayne's mom that "normal is relative." How do you think "normal" is different at Bayview compared to Sea Ridge Middle School? Is Jenika's normal the same as Rayne's? How might "normal" be different from person to person?

10. What lessons do Rayne's parents learn about their daughter over the course of the novel? What does Rayne learn about herself?

11. At the beginning of the book, Rayne wishes she could "stop everyone from noticing [her] hearing problem at all." How have her feelings started to change by the end of the book?

12. Why does Rayne end up admiring Helen Keller? How does Helen's perspective help shift how Rayne thinks about herself and her hearing loss?

ACKNOWLEDGMENTS

This is the story I swore I'd never write. So it's only appropriate to begin my thank yous with Molly O'Neill. While discussing my hearing loss and books needing d/Deaf representation, Molly suggested that I write a story with hearing loss as a central theme. I wasn't having it; I didn't want a character's entire arc to revolve around this. And yet, the day after our conversation, the first chapter of this book came to me in detail. In all my revisions, that opening has hardly changed. So thank you, Molly, for your push.

Putting so much of my personal story on paper was both terrifying and therapeutic. I'm fortunate that my agent, Janine Le of the Sheldon Fogelman Agency, not only embraced Rayne's story, but championed it all the way to publication. There's no one I'd rather surf the sea of publishing with. To her and the entire SF literary team, my words feel inadequate, but I'm immeasurably grateful!

My brilliant editor, Amy Fitzgerald, loved this story from the beginning—and I do mean the beginning, when she critiqued ten pages of it at a Florida SCBWI conference. She understood the heart of Rayne's story and helped me clarify that on the page. Her word-wizardry made the book exponentially better, and the gift of working with her is like catching an epic wave and riding it all the way to shore.

Thank you to the incredible team at Lerner/ Carolrhoda Books who came together to make this story an actual book, including editorial assistant Em Prozinski, production designer Erica Johnson, book designer Emily Harris, and cover illustrator Robert Sae-Heng. I'm indebted to each of you for making this all I dreamed it would be.

This story would be seriously flawed without the expertise of so many who graciously answered my research questions. April Halle Esq. of The Halle Law Firm, PA, and Stacey Cohen Blass, Esq., of Cohen Blass Law, PA, provided knowledge of the Florida legal system that ensured a necessary accuracy for this story. I appreciate Gigi Kean for connecting me with them. The National Institute on Deafness and Other Communication Disorders hosts a thoroughly detailed website (https://www.nidcd.nih.gov/) and granted me permission to use their name in this book. People across multiple cochlear implant, hard of hearing, and d/Deaf groups offered advice and answered questions. Their stories brought authenticity to this book in ways I could never have foreseen and certainly couldn't have otherwise written. Tina Morris, whose son is bilaterally implanted, was an invaluable resource on implant surgery and the benefits of CIs. Thank you, Ernie Kapanke, for introducing us. Sandra Prentiss, my own cochlear implant audiologist at the University of Miami, is a gem and a wealth of information. She provided last-minute details during my revision. My son, Griffin, is a gaming expert, and his knowledge helped me craft Troy's storyline realistically. Money well spent, after all. Each one of these people allowed me to add rich layers to Rayne's story. May they all know how infinitely thankful I am for their help.

I never would have been able to do this story justice without an in-person visit to a school designed for d/Deaf students. I was certain I knew the ending of this book after I'd written Chapter 1, but that all changed when I visited the Florida School for the Deaf and Blind in St. Augustine, Florida. Rick Coleman gave me an in-depth tour and invited me to watch a talent show that day. Since I had trouble hearing him on the group tour, he allowed me to sit one-on-one with him afterward as he answered the countless questions of this wide-eyed author. Forever grateful!

Dr. Fred Rahe was not only my audiologist for years, but he's also now a dear friend. His wisdom is much appreciated, especially in his role as an expert and beta reader for this novel. Cheers!

Maria and Dave Cathcart are childhood friends of mine and proofreading geniuses. I'm humbled by their pure excitement to read my almost-finished work and offer edits. Many, many thanks!

Being my most personal story yet, this book brought out much emotion for me during the writing process. I'm blessed with the best critique group (L2W) in the universe. Each of them held my hand as I navigated Rayne's journey to self-acceptance on the page. I was able to push forward thanks to their patience, guidance, and spot-on advice. For over fifteen years these kick-butt girls—Michelle

Delisle, Jill Mackenzie, Kristina Miranda, Meredith McCardle, and Ty Shiver—have been my rocks. My love, gratitude, and admiration for them cannot be put into words. You girls are the Jenika to my Rayne!

My parents, my biggest cheerleaders, are always excited to read my newest stories. I'll never be able to thank them enough for allowing me to dream big and for teaching me to have unwavering faith in all things.

Of course, I must thank my pups for their crazy escapades, which usually end up in the pages of my books. Special gratitude for Duke and Lucky who listened to me read this story aloud countless times as I wrote and revised. Note to self: use generic dog names in the book so as not to confuse your real dogs when reading out loud.

A huge shout-out to my kids, Kylie, Josh, and Griffin, for the incredible joy they bring me and for loving and supporting me always—even when I've embarrassed them with my hearing-hiccups in public. They are, without a doubt, the waves that keep me riding. Love, love, and more love!

My husband, Shawn, is a special human in more ways than I could ever put into words. My writing career, much like my hearing loss journey, has been a rollercoaster, but I'm so glad he's remained strapped beside me for the ride. Love, always!

Above all else, I thank God . . . for *always* steering my board.

ABOUT THE AUTHOR

Kerry O'Malley Cerra is the author of the multi-award-winning middle-grade novel *Just a Drop of Water*. She holds a degree in social science education and currently works as a high school media specialist. She spends her days enveloped by books and students and spends her nights writing by the glow of her computer. Though she'll always consider South Jersey/Philly her home, she currently lives in Florida with her family and two poorly behaved rescue dogs. Be sure to pop over to KerryOmalleyCerra.com and say hi!